Praise for Lilah Suzanne

BROKEN RI...

"TOP PICK! This excellent take on the celebrity-and-normal-person romance moves at a fast clip while satisfying at every turn."

—*RT Book Reviews*

"Hollywood style meets Nashville charm in this sweet, sexy fling turned romance."

—*Publishers Weekly*

BURNING TRACKS

"FOUR STARS… *Burning Tracks* is a deeply emotional work that explores love, loss, risk and the struggles of commitment and self-sabotage. In the first book, readers were introduced to a new love, but in this book, readers observe an established relationship. This makes *Burning Tracks* a fundamentally different read from its predecessor, both in tone and in what's at stake for our heroines."

—*RT Book Reviews*

SPICE

"… Completely laugh-out-loud funny and the underlying romantic plot is the perfect backdrop for its sparkling characters, Simon and Benji, who are bound to induce a book hangover… Fresh, fun fiction at its best!"

—*RT Book Reviews*

"Suzanne keeps the humor warm and the sex real."

—*Publishers Weekly*

PIVOT AND SLIP

"4.5 stars… Balancing laughter with touching emotions, this novella is a great first effort."

—*Carly's Book Reviews Blog*

BLENDED NOTES

BOOK THREE IN THE *SPOTLIGHT* SERIES

interlude  **press** • new york

ISBN (trade): 978-1-945053-23-8
ISBN (ebook): 978-1-945053-40-5
Published by Interlude Press
www.interludepress.com
Book Design by CB Messer with Lex Huffman
Cover Illustration by Victoria S. with CB Messer
Cover Design by CB Messer

10 9 8 7 6 5 4 3 2 1

interlude ✿ press • new york

"Always be true to yourself, what you believe, and where you came from... you'll need those roots sooner or later."
—*Dolly Parton*

1

Grady's earliest memory of his mother is watching her leave. It wasn't the first time she dropped him off at Memaw and Granddaddy's house, and the remembered moment itself is unremarkable: He's standing by the road; a cloud of dirt from the driveway into the trailer park lingers hazily in the air; he can see the taillights of her car lit red at the stop sign. The right one blinks a signal, the car turns, and she's gone. Memaw came to collect him soon after, and he doesn't recall what he did next—whatever rambunctious five-year-old boys like to do. Maybe he got on his bike and tore around the neighborhood, training wheels be damned. Or maybe he found a squirrel to harass with a makeshift slingshot of forked stick and rubber band. Maybe Memaw plunked him down in front of their old jumpy television.

Sit down for five seconds, Grady. Land's sake! she'd say, with a look rather similar to the one Nico has when Grady comes around to the aisle where Nico is browsing for home decor. Grady had wandered off when he spotted an old gramophone on display.

"There you are."

"Here I am," Grady confirms, dropping a kiss onto Nico's cheek. Nico leans into him with an easy, comfortable affection that grounds Grady, makes him feel wanted and safe. Grady takes a clear glass bottle from the shelf filled with clear glass bottles of all shapes and sizes and colors and asks, "Do we need apothecary jars?" The label on the jar reads: *Green Pain Pills.*

Nico takes the jar and turns, holding it up so it catches the sunlight streaming through the plate glass windows in the front of the boutique. "I mean, we don't *not* need apothecary jars." He tips his head and narrows his eyes, assessing the jar before putting it back on the shelf. Nico is determined to fill their new home with things that represent them; it's sweet, but, for Grady, unnecessary. Nico expresses himself visually: his clothes, his hair, the elegant yet assertive way he holds himself. Of course he'd want knickknacks and furniture and art that speak to the life they're building together. For Grady, it's less tangible, not a particular thing he could put on a shelf. It's two toothbrushes in the holder, the sound of a familiar car pulling into the garage, the lingering scent of Nico's cologne in their bed, the way Nico brushes a peck to Grady's lips before he leaves: never a goodbye, always a see you later.

"Did you find something you wanted?" Nico moves on to a display of antique paperweights. One looks like a crystal ball.

"Oh, yeah." Grady lifts his eyebrows and quirks his lips. Nico shakes his head at that, picks up the crystal ball paperweight, and passes it slowly from hand to hand. "I knew you were going to say that and yet—"

"And yet you still asked," Grady finishes, teasing, "Why, I think you may even like it."

Nico hums. He puts the paperweight back. "I suppose I must, considering that I am marry—" He snaps his mouth shut, then glances around to be sure no one overheard him. They're alone in the store, but still Nico mouths the end of that sentence: "*Marrying you.*"

And, lord, but does that thrill Grady to his bones, silent or spoken or acted out with charades. He's marrying Nico, they're getting married, he and Nico are *marrying each other.* Grady can tell his own smile is goofy, and Nico has one to match. In the quiet corner of this very unusual store, they can be openly giddy—for a moment.

The front door to the shop swings open, and a large group of people comes clamoring inside. He and Nico go back to browsing separately: Nico at a wall of picture frames; Grady at a table with porcelain doll parts spread across it. He picks up a pair of arms with a price tag of seventy-five dollars. What would Memaw have to say about such things? Grady sets the arms back down, nothing good, he bets. Boy, would she ever love Nico, though.

"The invitations should be ready by now." Nico strides past him, already heading to the door. "We should go pick them up, then straight home. I want to get started right away." Nico's shoulders are high and pulled back; his words are crisp. When it comes to wedding planning, he goes into full-on taskmaster mode.

"Yes, sir," Grady drawls, happy to follow along.

Back at home, after painstakingly addressing a stack of envelopes, Nico is low on patience and not very pleased with the derisive snort he gets in response when he asks where he should send an invitation for Grady's mother.

Grady doesn't remember crying over his mama leaving back then or any other time. It was normal, the calamity she brought to their lives, and no one in that trailer ever talked about it. Memaw and Granddaddy didn't know any more than he did about where she was going, what she was doing, or when she'd be back. So they carried on as usual, and it's only in retrospect that Grady's connected the dots between her leaving and his getting in trouble at school or at home or, later on, turning tail and running whenever his personal relationships got difficult. He's still fighting that reflex now.

"Even if I did know where she was, she wouldn't show," Grady explains in the office of their new house.

Nico is at the old-fashioned rolltop desk in a state-of-the-art ergonomic chair. The realtor described this house as city-sleek-meets-rustic-charm, and that about sums it up for the house and everything in it, including them. Nico taps a neat pile of robin's-egg blue envelopes even neater. "Okay, but don't you think she'd at least want to know? Whether she shows up or not? We're keeping everything so hush-hush, she won't find out otherwise."

She gave him two birthday presents during his entire life: A metal Tonka truck and a pair of snakeskin cowboy boots. The boots she brought in person when he was nine. She took him to McDonald's for lunch and let him pick anything he wanted to eat, and then he opened the present right there in the plastic booth. He remembers bouncing around as if he were filled with his soda's fizzing bubbles, giggly and giddy, as he admired the boots. When he looked up to thank her, she shook her head.

"You look just like your daddy," she told him. "God help us all."

In the office, Grady gives up trying to get comfortable in the oblong molded-fiberglass rocking chair—he still has a hard time wrapping his brain around furniture that's really decoration and decoration that's really furniture—and stands behind Nico.

4

"I don't know where she is," he repeats, instead of providing an answer to the question of whether or not his own mother would care that he's getting married. He doesn't know. She very well may not, and that's something Nico can't quite understand.

"How about your dad?"

Grady laughs, and Nico gives him a sharp look that is less irritation at Grady and more dismay that Grady's own parents truly do not care one whit about him. "Sweetheart," Grady says and rubs at the tense pull of muscles across Nico's shoulders. "I appreciate what you're trying to do, but it's not necessary. I'll have my family there. Clem, Flora and Gwen and Cayo, my band, Spencer." Nico's shoulders pull tighter at Spencer's name. "Your mom and dad and brother," Grady continues, massaging the knotted tendons at the base of Nico's neck. "Soon they'll be my family *officially*. I'm not sad or upset about anyone missing." Other than Memaw and Granddaddy, but of course that's a different kind of missing.

Nico's shoulders relax. "Okay."

"Okay." Grady's fingers drift up Nico's neck to brush the shells of his prominent ears. They've been wedding planning for hours now, hunkered down in the office checking things off lists, and it's making Grady restless. But when he bends to caress Nico's neck and ears with his lips, Nico catches him by the chin.

"Hold that thought. If I don't get these invitations addressed and out today, I will lose it."

Grady pouts and stands up. "Anything I can do?"

Nico uncaps a pen with decisive force. "You can stand there and look handsome."

"Done." Grady wanders to the bookshelf. In the corner he spots a ukulele that went missing a few weeks ago and strums a bit of his new single.

Once in a life, a boy comes along
And blows your world apart

It would have been better if she had just disappeared. His grandparents were dedicated and loving, even though he had been dumped on their doorstep. They didn't have much, but he never went without, never felt lacking or unstable. Then his mother would blow into town like a storm—or, more rarely, his father—and he'd be shaken to pieces. And the very worst part is that when Mama was present, not just there, but sober, she was wonderful.

With a love that burns so bright

His mama was infused with light: bright and fun, at least she was when things were on an upswing in Lily's life. She took him to Pigeon Forge once, just the two of them, to Dollywood. They ate ice cream and went to the shows and on all the rides, the big scary ones, too, where she held his hand so he wouldn't be afraid. He remembers singing and laughing and raising their hands up high on the peak of a roller coaster. At age eleven, Grady knew what it felt like to be Icarus.

It shines a light
Through the cracks of your broken heart.

He always got burned, yet he never could convince himself that he was soaring headlong into the flames. *This time,* he'd think, *this time she'll stay.*

Grady's song trips into a minor key, so he sets the instrument down; there's nothing more depressing than a sad ukulele solo.

"Actually," Nico says, addressing an envelope in his careful, precise handwriting. "If I could see your contacts list... I don't have addresses for your band members."

"Then can we be done?" Only half paying attention, Grady thumbs through his contacts, then drops his phone onto the desk and slumps over it with a pleading look.

Nico cocks his head and arches a sharp eyebrow; it's dead sexy. "Good things come to those who wait."

Grady lets his voice slip low and dragging, "I do like the sound of that." He slinks closer, but is thwarted again when Nico leans away, intentionally out of reach.

Six months out, and Grady is fed up with wedding planning. He'd suggest they elope, only Nico's mother would be heartbroken, and Grady would never forgive himself for hurting that dear, sweet angel who loves him like her own. Besides, there is the honeymoon to look forward to: a private bungalow in an isolated tropical paradise that Grady's half-convinced they may never leave. That suits him just fine; he can make music anywhere, anytime, for anyone.

Two weeks later, the RSVPs are trickling in. They've kept the invitation list small, limited to people they can trust to not spill the beans to a tabloid, or in other words, not Spencer.

Grady has a meeting at his record company to finalize the new album; he's running out the door when an overnight envelope tips into the doorway. He doesn't think much of it until he starts to fling the letter inside for Nico to deal with and catches the name on the return address.

Clay Dawson.

2

"**Hey, Nico?**" **Grady** taps the thick envelope on his open palm while he waits with one foot inside the door, one out.

"Yes?" Nico enters the foyer fiddling with a tie knotted at his throat and his shirt still untucked.

Grady taps the envelope one last time, then holds it up in accusation. "What is this?"

Nico's fretful fingers pause on the perfectly done knot of his tie, and he arches one eyebrow. "That... is an envelope," he says, deadpan. "Is that all? Would you like me to identify the color of the sky for you as well?"

Normally Grady loves Nico's cutting sense of humor; a cantankerous icy facade that hides the warm, kind inside, in the same way that each piece of his fastidiously chosen outfits is another link in his chainmail. Once he painstakingly chooses cufflinks or a collar-chain or the perfect Eldridge knot, Nico can face any challenge. Grady loves Nico's layers, loves even more that he gets to strip him of them, clothing and otherwise. But right now, Grady is really literally running out the door, and Nico is up to something.

"This is from Clay Dawson. My uncle. Why does my uncle have this address?" Any contact Grady had with his uncle was through his manager Vince.

Nico's mouth forms a little "o" shape, and, purposely avoiding Grady, he turns to the mirror in the entryway to finish tying his tie. He knows why, and he knows that Grady knows why, and they keep butting up against this, don't they? Nico decides what's best and doesn't give Grady a chance at an opinion. Every step of the way on this relationship, Grady had to prove that he really does want this and he really does know what he's doing. Nico is worth the patience; he's worth Grady's struggle against his own instinct to cut and run because that would be easier, for both of them. It'd be easier still to drop the conversation, ditch the letter in the trash, and walk out the door. Grady moves his other foot back inside and lets the door fall closed. "You sent him a wedding invite."

"No." Nico smooths his eyebrows in the mirror, casual-like. "*Technically* I sent your father an invite. You don't have his address, but I assumed Uncle Clay would get it to him."

Grady flicks the letter onto their sideboard. It lands halfway on the specially commissioned copper dish that holds Nico's keys and wallet, a pack of gum, and three nickels. "I don't—I'm gonna be late for a meeting. I can't deal with this right now."

"Grady—"

He shoves the door open; he plants both feet on the porch this time. "You know, every once in while I may actually know what's best. My father is bad person, Nico. I don't mean like he's a bad tipper or he litters in the park. I mean lying, cheating, and stealing from everyone he knows. I mean prison. Dangerous, Nico."

"I'm sorry. I didn't know." Nico does look genuinely remorseful. He didn't know because Grady hasn't been entirely forthcoming about his past. He wants to leave it there, in the *past*, where it belongs. Whatever anger was reaching a boil in his blood simmers down; he never can stay angry with Nico for long. He doesn't have time to settle things between them in any conclusive way, though. He really is running late. So he deflates, sighing and crooking his finger to beckon Nico closer until Grady can pull him in by the tie.

"I just got that knot right," Nico protests, but definitely does not protest the kiss Grady lays on him, responding eagerly with parting lips, bending his long, lithe body into Grady's.

Grady pulls away with regret, darting in for one last parting peck on Nico's soft lips. "I really have to go. We'll talk about this later. In the meantime, do not contact any more of my estranged relatives, if you can manage it."

Nico nods, then lifts his chin. "Okay, but what about estranged friends? Estranged coworkers?" He wiggles grasping fingers in the air. "There has to be some kind of meddling I can do." Grady's mouth slips into a smile—he never can help it—then he jogs down the steps. "We'll talk later."

It's been a long time since Grady first came through the rotating doors of Stomp Records awed and nervous and still convinced someone there had made a huge mistake in offering him a record deal. His boots clack on the marble floors and echo through the expansive lobby. He passes the front desk, where he's waved right through, and takes an elevator that plays someone else's latest hit. Sometimes it plays his, he knows, and elevator music wasn't ever really a goal of his, but there it is anyway.

He's not nervous today, and hasn't been for a long time. It's not that he doesn't care, or that he's no longer astounded by what he's achieved. The only way to stay sane, he's found, is to be completely underwhelmed by own his success. "Grady Dawson the country star" is an entity that was created here, that lives here, part of Grady, but not him, not really. Grady cares about music. Everything else is the label's deal.

"Grady." Vince meets Grady by the tenth floor reception desk. His manager has less hair every time Grady sees him.

"Vinny!" Grady claps him on the back. Vince wheezes and fumbles his briefcase.

"Listen, Grady. I wanted to talk with you before we—"

"Mr. Delmont will see you now," the receptionist interrupts.

Grady leans over the high desk embossed with Stomp Records' logo in gold. "Thank you, Doris." Doris has worked for Duke Delmont, an executive at Stomp Records, for as long as Grady has been signed with them, and she's been mentioning retirement "any day now" for just as long. She's a doll; Grady loves seeing her sweet face here whenever he comes in. "Something is different about you," Grady says, leaning closer to get a better look at her. "Don't tell me."

"Grady," Vince hisses, trying to regain Grady's attention.

"New lipstick," Grady says, waving to Vince that he's coming. "No. Your hair?"

Doris frets and blushes and touches her curled gray hair. "Well, I did get this fancy new face cream."

"That's it." Grady snaps his fingers. "It's working for you. And here I thought you couldn't get any prettier."

Doris giggles and blushes and swats at him, "Oh, you charmer."

"*Grady.*"

He says goodbye to Doris, then hustles to catch up to Vince down a wide thickly carpeted hallway. Vince is a great guy and good manager, but he worries too much. Grady should send him on vacation before his next tour starts.

"About the new single," Vince says in that same harsh whisper. "I want to make sure that you and I are on the same—"

"Grady, my boy!"

Duke Delmont has the look of a man who never denies himself the very best in life. Broad-shouldered and barrel-chested, he has a deep, booming voice, slicked down white hair and is dressed to the nines in a shiny sharkskin suit, cowboy boots, and a huge gold-plated belt buckle with a bold silver "D" in the center: Duke certainly leaves a lasting impression. Grady always wants to bring Nico along to these meetings and watch his reactions to Duke Delmont and his flashy approach to style; he can just imagine the flicker of disapproval in Nico's eyes about that shiny silver suit.

"Duke, good to see you; thanks for meeting with me." They shake hands, and Duke ushers them inside to the leather chairs in the center of his huge window-walled office. A view of Music Row spreads out on the street beneath them. They're in the center of the chugging, churning engine of country music here: the labels, studios, production stages, radio networks and stations, magazines and websites, and a few dedicated TV stations.

"My boy, my boy. No need for the formalities!" Duke chortles. "How've you been?"

Duke is loud and blustering, rich and powerful beyond anything Grady could ever imagine, yet he's been there for Grady's whole journey here in Nashville: the highs and the ugly, rock-bottom lows. He's been disappointed in Grady and warned him that the label might drop him if he doesn't get it together, but even when it took Grady a few tries, Duke never gave up on him, never did drop him from the label. And now?

"I'm… really great, actually, I—" He starts to tell Duke about Nico, about his new home and family, how he's getting married to this imperfect, gorgeous, frustrating, *amazing* man, and Grady has never been happier—even in their bad moments, he is so, so happy.

Duke barges ahead before he can say anything. "Good, great, look I'ma go ahead here. I don't want to waste your time, Grady."

Vince shifts forward and back in his seat; he seems even more stressed out than usual. What was he trying to tell Grady? What does he know that Grady doesn't? This is supposed to be a quick stamp of approval on the single, with maybe a few minor tweaks. Then Duke will insincerely ask Grady to play a game of golf, and Grady will give his sincere regrets, and they'll part ways until next time.

"You know I think your stuff is just fantastic, you know that. Some people," Duke sweeps his right hand out, vaguely indicating the rest of the building outside of his office. On his pinky is a huge gold ring. "*Some people.* Not me, I would never, you know that. They think the single is too controversial. Too political."

Grady furrows his brows. Controversial? "How— I don't— It's a love song. How is that political?"

Duke says nothing, but takes a little silver remote from a side table and presses a button. Grady's new song fills the office.

I know this isn't your average love song
But this is not an average love

It's good. Really good. Or so he thought. Was he wrong? To him it sounds raw and real and honest about being in love, really and truly in lasting love. How could that be controversial? Unless—Oh. *Political.* Grady's blood flares hot; his fingers clench tight on the leather arms on his oversized chair. He glances at Vince, who begs with his eyes and the flat line of his mouth for Grady to let him handle it, but rage boils over.

"I'm surprised at you, Duke. I didn't take you for a coward. A few people clutch their Sunday pearls, and you roll over to show your belly, that easy?"

Sometimes he can almost hear the trampled remnants of Vince's patience cry out for mercy. "What Grady means, Duke," Vince says through clenched teeth. "Is that Grady's, er, lifestyle—" Grady makes an offended noise of protest. "Grady's *personal relationships,*" Vince amends, "Haven't been an issue before, and we're not quite sure why it matters all of a sudden."

Grady defiantly crosses his arms, but he gives Vince an approving nod.

"Grady, Grady," Duke says, as soothing as his harsh, booming voice can manage. "This isn't coming from me. You know I'm a huge champion of equal rights. Hell, I made a donation recently! A big one. You know me! But I have to consider other people. I'm not running a kingdom here; I ain't supreme ruler!" He chortles again, it sets Grady's teeth on edge. "Your, uh. Your fella. What's his…"

"Nico."

"Nico. Well, you and Nico, you have to think about each other, right? Hey, I'm married, I get it. Can't be all about yourself now, right? So the single gets held up, then the album, then all of sudden they're talking breach of contract, they're talking lawsuits. You know that's out of my hands, Grady, that's lawyer stuff. Then what? That affects Nico, too."

Grady shifts in his chair, looks from Duke to Vince, and Vince's eyebrows raise to his nonexistent hair line in a silent *how do you want to play this?* But Grady doesn't know. He's always had his integrity when he had nothing else, when his life was in shambles, even then he held fast to his vision and his honesty and never hid who he was or the men and women he dated and thought then that he loved. And now, now he has so much more.

"I'll, uh—" Grady's fingers refuse to loosen their viselike grip on the armrests, and anger simmers in his belly but he shakes his head and grits out, "I'll take another look at the song."

3

"That's bullshit."

"Gwen." Flora inclines her head and widens her eyes in Cayo's direction. The little guy is too busy gumming on a wooden block to listen to whatever the grownups are on about. Grady and Gwen are both cross-legged on the floor with him, and Flora is perched on the couch, guarding the glasses of lemonade on the coffee table from tiny grabbing hands.

"Well, it is…" Gwen retorts, but silently mouths the word this time. "*Bullshit.*"

"So they're refusing to release the song?" Flora asks. Grady came right to their house after the meeting with Duke. It's a good place to go when he needs a kind and understanding ear or two. That and Flora is great cook.

"Not exactly," Grady hedges. "They won't release it *as is*. They want me to make some changes."

"Changes as in: Make it about a girl, so no one's delicate sensibilities are offended, because it was only okay for you to be bi in theory, like that's the way it works, right? Gotta pick one or the other and *whoops,* you chose wrong." Gwen's arms flap wildly as she rants; she has such a loud presence for such a small person. Cayo crawls over and hands her the block, which is now covered in drool, as she finishes with a final, "Bullshit."

"Gwen. Do you want our child's first word to be—" She stage-whispers, "*bullshit.*"

Gwen scoops up Cayo, who squeals and grabs two handfuls of Gwen's purple and platinum blond pompadour. "He's the biracial adopted child of two lesbians in Tennessee. It'll probably come in handy." She covers his fat little cheeks in kisses and makes *nom-nom-nom* noises. "Isn't that right, Bubba?"

Smiling despite herself, Flora closes her eyes and tips her head back. She looks just like Grady's Memaw used to when she was asking the Lord to please give her strength. When she opens her eyes again Grady gives Flora a smile and wink, and she blushes prettily.

"My manager thinks I can just make the song vague instead of changing it." Drop the *he's and him's* for *you and yours.*" Still the same song, Vince argued, just more palatable. *Play the game, Grady; it sucks, but you don't have much recourse here.*

Gwen's right, it is bullshit.

Cayo crawls over to Grady, then pulls himself up on the coffee table to grab the pretty glasses. He's steady on his feet now as long as he's holding on to something; he'll be walking any day—growing too fast. Flora deftly moves the glasses out of the way, and Grady picks up a nearby board book to distract Cayo with.

"In the great green room," Grady reads. Cayo plunks himself down on Grady's bent right knee. "There was a telephone. And a red balloon. And a picture of—" Cayo settles in against Grady's chest and his wispy, wild curls tickle Grady's chin. He couldn't adore this child more than if he were his own; he just loves him clear to bits. Is that how Grady's grandparents felt? That instead of being the burden Grady always felt he was, he was a surprising blessing, just as Cayo is? "—and a comb and brush and a bowl full of mush. And a quiet old lady who was whispering *hush*." When Cayo makes a *shh* sound along with the narration, Grady presses a grin into his hair.

"And what happens if you refuse?" Flora asks when the book is finished and has become a teething toy like the block. "Can you just... Not change it?"

"Yeah, fu—I mean *eff* the man!" Gwen adds.

"Yeah, sure," Grady agrees. "Only thing is they take breach of contract pretty seriously."

Flora frowns at that, and Gwen scowls. Cayo continues gnawing on *Goodnight Moon*. Now that he's talked it out with this family that knows sacrifice and compromise and that love requires setting aside ego and selfishness, Grady has an inkling of what he should do.

"What did Nico say?" Flora crouches in front of Cayo with a teething biscuit. It's dry-looking and cardboard-colored and can't taste much better than the book, Grady figures. Cayo takes the trade.

He hasn't told Nico because he knows Nico will tell him to stand his ground. Grady can imagine him, jaw set defiantly, spine held rigidly. He would never let Grady compromise who he is or his voice, but who Grady is comes at a cost to Nico. He sacrifices for Grady: his privacy, his career, where he lives, time with his family, time with Grady. And what does Grady sacrifice for him?

"I'm, uh, still workin' out what to tell him." Grady squirms under the matching looks of disapproval and concern Gwen and

Flora direct at him, but he's saved when Cayo drops his teething biscuit and makes another lunge for the glasses on the coffee table.

"I should head out." Grady hauls himself off the floor, drops kisses on three cheeks—one smeared with teething biscuit goop—it does taste like cardboard, matter of fact—and declines the offer to stay for dinner.

He means to go home, but finds himself rumbling in his truck down a side street in Music Row to an old brick cottage turned recording studio. It's sure not the large art-deco inspired state-of-the-art studio he's used to now. But as his boots echo across the plank flooring, which gives under his weight, the dark, cramped interior, whose walls are padded with cheap egg-carton foam insulation, it brings him right back to the first studio he worked in. Back then, he'd been so thrilled just to be there, he didn't care about his reputation or the number of albums he would sell or how to get his name in as many magazines as possible—and by any means necessary. He just wanted to make music. Has he lost his way, so determined to make something of himself and shed his past for good? Has his reputation become more important to him than simply doing his job by making a decent record?

Clementine waves to him from the soundboard. A slight young woman wearing a slouchy toboggan hat and a gray and orange University of Tennessee T-shirt is in the booth wearing headphones and studying sheet music. Grady's never seen her. She's cute, though Grady suspects he's not exactly her type.

"What are you doing here? And who is that?" When he called after leaving Gwen and Flora's to see what Clem was up to, this was not what he expected. Of course, with Clem he never did know what to expect.

"Borrowing some studio time from an associate," Clementine says to his first question, reaches across him to flip a switch, and to the second question replies, "That is Ellis Booker, and she's about to blow up Nashville." Clem starts the backing track, gives Ellis a signal, and the most hauntingly gorgeous blues voice comes out of her mouth.

Grady whistles. "Damn. Where did you find her?"

"At a... lady bar." Clem turns the music down and ignores Grady's delighted grin.

"And what were you doing at a *lady bar*?"

Clem flips tousled copper-gold waves and adjusts a few things on the soundboard. "I do not have to explain myself to you, Grady Dawson."

Grady laughs. "All right. So you picked up this cute girl, at a *lady bar*, took her home, and found out she could *sang*."

"You would go there," she says, with a fond shake of her head. "No, she was setting up for the headliner, whom I was actually there to see. I wasn't even really paying attention to her; she was just doing a sound check. Then that *voice*." She pushes a few controls high up on the soundboard and nudges one down. Clem has always taken a big part in producing her own songs, but this is new. "I had to talk to her and found out she'd been rejected all over town because she didn't have the right 'look.' And I just thought it was criminal. This level of talent, and she's working tech at a bar because she's not a buxom blonde in cowboy boots?"

It is criminal, and exactly describes Clementine's look early in her career. How many of them have had to twist and contort themselves for their dreams?

"I may have a knack for developing talent," Clem continues. "I mean, once upon a time there was this scruffy, curly haired disaster that I nurtured into a bona fide superstar." She nudges him with her elbow. He would take offense at being called a disaster, but...

His music has always been real, raw, honest. Yet where would he be without cleaning up his act? Off the map like his mother? Jail and then crashing on couches like his father until people got sick of him? Worse?

"Duke wants me to change the single. Says it's too controversial for country music. I don't know what to do."

Clementine looks at him as if she has X-ray vision that scans past his skin and bones and guts right to his heart. "I think you do."

Grady leans back in the chair and watches Ellis sing her soul out. Her hands hold the headphones tightly; her eyes are clenched shut. Success, Grady has learned in the years since he wandered awestruck into a crumbling old studio for the first time, before he was signed, before anyone cared about him or who he was, has precious little to do with raw talent. "Everyone compromises," he says finally.

"Sure," Clem signs a thumbs up to Ellis. "But your name will be on that album, not Duke's. So what you have to ask yourself is, does it sound like you or your compromises?"

4

He means to go home after leaving the studio, he really does. Nico is home by now for sure. He heads that way, toward their house hidden in the forested hills rising around the edge of downtown Nashville. But when he's stopped at a red light, his fingers drum on the steering wheel, and his left legs jogs up and down. He gets the familiar sensation that his skin is too tight and his mind is zipping from thought to thought to thought as if the cable's gone out so only static and jumping colors and squiggling lines and noise are left on the screen. He needs to clear his head.

"Yo, Grady! Wassup?"

"Benny, how's it, man?"

"Excellent." Benny comes from behind the counter with his hand held low. Grady connects their palms in a low-five, then pulls Benny in for a half hug. It's nice to have someone greet him like that, happy to see him, *him,* just Grady, and actually mean it. It's one of the reasons this dirt bike track in the boonies is a sanctuary, where he can shed his mask and put the weight on his shoulders aside for a spell.

Benny checks Grady in, then puts his locker key on the motor-oil-smeared countertop and says in one breath, "Yo, I know you like those beast machines, but I have this spankin' new Husqvarna two-stroke 125cc, if you wanna hit those fat jumps like I know you do." Benny is baby-faced and excited and wears sleeveless shirts to show off his fully tatted arms and a sideways baseball cap with shaggy brown hair fringed beneath it. He's worked at the dirt bike track for a couple years now: awesome kid.

Grady slips the locker key into his pocket and stops to try out the new bike still sitting pristine in the office. "Mm, all right." Grady grips the handlebars and shifts the body left to right. "Put it out for me while I change?"

Benny grins. "Yeah, of course man! It's tight, right?"

Grady agrees, then swings a leg over the bike to sit sidesaddle. "Benny, lemme ask you somethin'. If your boss came to you and said that you had to… I dunno. Wear long sleeves and cover up your tattoos. Like you can keep 'em, that's fine, but you have to hide 'em. Would you?"

"Ah, shit, uh." Benny lifts the brim of his hat up, then tugs it low. "I mean. I'd wanna say take it or leave it, this is me, you know? But I got bills to pay, yo. Know what I mean?" He laughs. Grady frowns and looks away.

"Yeah, I know what you mean."

A friendly hand squeezes Grady's shoulder. "Hey, man, whatever's got you down, go leave it out there on the track, yeah?"

He tries to.

The sun is orange and so low it looks as if it's resting on the treetops when Grady finally drives up their steep, winding driveway.

He is more calm and clearheaded, even if he still doesn't know what to do. Nico's car is parked in the garage, and the door is unlocked, but the house is quiet. The ground level is taken up by a practice space and a home gym and the garage. The second floor, accessed outside by the front deck and inside by the first set of stairs, is the kitchen, living room, dining room, and whatever that room with the massive stone fireplace and insanely expensive furniture is named. "Sitting room" the realtor called it. They never sit there. Two large bedrooms and their office are up another flight of stairs.

Grady already has his shirt off, heading right to the shower, when he spots Nico in the kitchen. He's sorting through mail at the breakfast bar with his tie pulled loose, shirt sleeves rolled up his forearms, and the top two buttons of his collar tugged open. The setting sun catches his face, highlighting the sharp lines of his cheekbones and jaw, tinting his eyes even darker in shadow, and bronzing his skin with golden light. Grady's breath leaves his body in a sigh, and in its place is yearning for Nico, just like the first time he saw him, just like every time he sees him still.

Grady sidles up behind him and wraps his arms around his waist, and Nico's only acknowledgment is the quirk of one eyebrow. Grady brushes a kiss onto the corner of his jaw.

"You smell like dirt and gasoline," Nico says. He rips open an envelope, glances over the letter, then tosses it on the smaller pile.

Grady kisses down the back of his neck. "And sweat."

"Mm." Nico opens another letter and tilts his head, silent encouragement for Grady's mouth to continue. Nico leans his weight into Grady, back to chest, ass to pelvis, and Grady goes for the big guns, nipping at his earlobe and earning a groan. He loves that trick.

"Wait." Nico smacks him lightly on the temple with a letter. "For you."

Grady doesn't recognize the name and opens it cautiously while Nico turns around. "It's a fan letter," Grady says.

"That's what I thought it was."

"But how did they find—"

"Exactly." Nico crosses his arms and leans back on the quartz-topped breakfast bar separating the kitchen and living room. "If it's a request for a lock of your hair again, we're moving. I don't care if we've only lived here for a few months."

It's not, just a regular fan letter—a pretty innocent one at that. He shows Nico. Still, somehow their address got out, and that's worrying enough on its own. "I'll have Vince do something. Give the address they can write to, out on the uh—" He snaps his fingers. "The tweet thing."

"You mean Twitter, Grandpa?" Nico's arms are still crossed, but he's smiling now. Teasing Grady always cheers him right up.

"Sure, whatever. I'm gonna shower."

Nico's arms drop, and he glances from Grady to the mail pile. Under what looks like the "keep" pile is the still unopened overnighted letter from his Uncle Clay. They have to talk about that. And they have to talk about his meeting with Duke. But Nico's eyes drag up and down Grady's body, lingering on his abdominals, then the mirrored pair of Swallows he had inked on his pecs in Vegas that Nico likes to trace with his fingers and lips and the tip of his tongue. Nico juts out a hip, his eyebrows rise and fall once. "Want company?"

This house is the ideal city location with a country feel. It mixes both of their styles, has space for Grady's cars and trucks and ATVs and a closet big enough for Nico's clothes and shoes. Plus, it already had a rehearsal space that could fit all of Grady's instruments with room for more. That the shower seems designed for shower sex— the size of a small room with double waterfall shower heads on opposite stone walls, multiple jets below, and a boulder fashioned as a curved seat—was a happy bonus.

In the shower, Grady picks up where he left off: pressed behind Nico, making a path along Nico's shoulders and neck and jaw and ears with his mouth. But now no clothes separate them, Nico's skin is not just a tease at his forearms and clavicle, and Grady runs his hands slick with soap everywhere he can reach: the solid muscles of Nico's chest; his narrow, angled hips and his long thighs; the tight, lean lines of his back and the perfect firm handfuls of his ass. Hot water runs in rivulets over them; soap bubbles twist down the drain. Grady pulls one of Nico's earlobes into his mouth, then reaches around to finally pay attention to his cock.

"Fuck. *Ah.*" Nico's hands slap onto the stone shower wall in front of him. His head drops, his hips rock, and Grady knows just how to get him off now, where to twist his grip, what pace gets Nico there right away and what winds him up slowly, where to rub and tease the head, and just what to say that gets him there every time. "That's right, sweetheart," Grady says, low and sex-graveled. He hooks his chin over Nico's shoulder to watch the rapid jerk of his own hand. "So gorgeous, come for me, sweetheart, come on." Nico reaches back and grabs a fistful of Grady's hair, making Grady's scalp sting sharply. He yelps and grinds his cock between the globes of Nico's ass, and Nico comes, shooting across the natural earth-tone stone tiles.

Nico recovers still braced against the wall in front of him, then manhandles Grady onto the boulder chair, drops to his knees, and seals his lips over Grady's stiff cock. Nico takes him apart as no one ever has, sucking him down with a single-minded focus that makes Grady dizzy. Nico makes love the way he does everything else: He's committed, determined, tenacious, and hell-bent on excellence. More than that, he touches Grady as though Grady is something worth giving his all. Nico looks at Grady as though he's something special.

Grady can't get enough of him; he is everything Grady never thought he could have.

After showering, Nico dresses in his fancy linen lounge pants and a supersoft organic cotton T-shirt. Grady doesn't dress at all—fresh air is good for the skin and other parts—just relaxes on the bed nude while Nico rambles about his day and plays with Grady's hair, and Grady's as content as a piglet in a puddle, can't even care about the song or Duke or anything. For dinner they decide to grill something and enjoy their new back veranda with its view of the downtown skyline, even though the heat is lingering humidly long into the evening.

Nico opens the sliding glass door just enough to stick his head out and ask, "Do you want to at least open this letter and see what he has to say before I toss it out?"

Grady moves cuts of salmon around on the grill. "Nope."

Nico's head ducks back inside. It pops back out again. "Okay, what if—"

"Nico," Grady warns, taking a pull from his soda can.

"Yes, okay, no meddling, sorry." His head pops in, then out again. Grady laughs at him, despite his annoyance. "I'm just—" he says.

"My father wants money. He was crashing with Clay last I knew because no one else can stand him any longer and he needs more money."

Nico nods, but still holds the envelope out, as if he can't quite make himself believe that.

Grady shakes his head, then lifts the salmon steaks to check for doneness—not yet. He's in a mellow mood with a cold drink and a warm summer evening and a fantastic orgasm still singing through his body, so fine. "Sweetheart, if it's bothering you that much, you can open it."

Nico's eyes light up. "Really?" He's setting himself up for disappointment, but if it's really that important, and it did come from a good place of genuine love and concern, then, "Really."

Grady finishes his soda, flips the salmon, and puts on asparagus spears to sear. They're not far from the city, yet it's so quiet and still. They have a clear view of the city on one side and trees everywhere else. They can fit quite a lot of people on this veranda, too. Maybe they could just have the wedding reception out here.

"Grady…"

Not just his head popped out of the sliding door, but Nico's whole body is outside. Grady's so excited to tell him about his idea for the reception that he just blurts it out without stopping to acknowledge the broken expression on Nico's face.

"Grady, I…"

The salmon is starting to char, one asparagus spear slips between the grates, falls into the flames, turns black. Nico holds out an unfolded piece of yellow paper.

"Grady. Your dad died."

5

Grady. *It's hard* *to get ahold of you. Hate to tell you this but Vaughn died last winter. Hope you are well. Sorry to bring bad news. Congratulations on the wedding.*

Clay Dawson

"How are you holding up?" Gwen says around several pins clenched between her teeth. She's crouched in front of the stool he's standing very, very still on, slipping one pin at a time along the inseam of his pants. He usually avoids answering questions when sharp pins are that close to his jewels, but, "I'm fine," he answers quickly and quietly.

Gwen stands. She seems even shorter than usual, and Grady fights the urge to pat her cute lil' head. He's glad he didn't, because she's sticking pins in the shirt along his side, very close to one nipple. "Fine, huh? Hold your arms out."

When she looks up at him, her eyes are filled not with mirth and teasing like usual, but with concern. Grady sighs. "He told you."

"Well, you know Nico and his constant oversharing of his personal life." She quips, then sticks a pin right below his armpit. "He told me your dad died, that's all. He didn't go into details."

"There aren't any details," Grady says. She doesn't push or prod, just finishes the tugging and pinning and folding on his clothes. Nico wouldn't leave it alone; he kept looking at Grady with sad eyes and a deep-set frown, poured mug after mug of hot tea for him, and asked if he needed anything and what he wanted to do. And then Nico's mom, with her mom ESP, got in on the action and called Grady to make sure he was okay. He had to talk her out of catching the first flight out of Sacramento. He's fine. He didn't even know the guy. He's surprised his father managed to live this long. "I'm fine," he tells Gwen again.

"Okay," she says, with a lilt of skepticism in her voice. "All done. Careful taking it off."

Grady tiptoes behind the changing screen with arms and legs held wide as if he's a puppet with tangled strings. He's in the office to get fitted for a custom suit, for once not for a photoshoot or interview or red carpet. For his wedding, he's getting a stand-in suit measured and tailored so the wedding suit will be a perfect fit on the big day. He just has to watch his soda intake until then. He's buoyant with excitement. Nico is working a video shoot, so he'll be away from the office all day. They've decided not to see each other's suits before the big day.

"Swatch time!" Gwen says when Grady is back in his jeans and Henley. He's tugging his boots on as Gwen hauls out a huge binder of fabric samples. It's full of satiny blacks and blues and more blacks. He's sure Nico would know the precise and vital differences between all of them, but to Grady they're boring.

"Can't Nico pick for me?" He probably wants them to coordinate, and Grady might pick a suit that clashes with Nico's.

"He was adamant that you pick one yourself, actually." Gwen heaves the binder over, so Grady can look from back to front. There is a wider variety of colors and patterns in the back. Grady peruses them, pleased that Nico listened to him, and that he's trying. "He said something about steamrolling you a lot lately," Gwen informs him. "Which I hoped was a sex position. He was also adamant that it was not."

The mirth is back in her eyes, and Grady laughs. Sometimes it's as if he and Gwen are the same person, as if she's a tiny female version of him with a filthy mind and filthier mouth. "If it's not a sex position it should be."

"Right? Hmm, what about houndstooth?"

Grady runs his fingers over the thick, black and white checked fabric. "It's usually still warm here in October. Might be too heavy?"

"That's true." She flips through more samples, scrunches her nose, and twists her lips. Her bony little shoulder presses into his side. He loves her—the sister he never had.

"Hey, Short Stuff. Wanna be my best woman?"

She drops the fabric in her hand to punch his arm. "Grady! Of course I will. Oh, man, your bachelor party is gonna be *epic.*"

Grady has a flash of regret; she's mostly bark, though he knows better than to say that out loud. Telling Gwen she can't do something is a guarantee she'll find a way do it.

They turn back to fabric samples. "What about green and blue?" Grady wonders. "Would that work as a tux?" There's a swatch of hunter green, it reminds Grady of the scarf Nico commissioned the first time he came to Nashville, when he was just a temporary stylist for Grady. Grady was so gone for Nico even then, it was torture being around him and not able to touch and kiss him.

"I think so," Gwen says. "We could do something like this." She flips to a lightweight gray fabric with subtle lines of blue. "Only a light green plaid with hunter green buttons and lapel." She takes out her phone to jot some things down and says, "Actually, that would go perfectly with—" She snaps her mouth closed.

"What?"

"I've said too much. Are you hungry?"

Nico G Style Studio is in a hip neighborhood that used to be abandoned warehouses and defunct manufacturing plants. Grady grew up in a little town south of the city, only coming into Nashville proper for school field trips and concerts and summer music festivals. The industrial setting in this area feels a lot like home. It's a working class town that will always be part of who he is, no matter how much of the world he sees.

Is his father buried back in their hometown?

"Not hungry?"

They picked a restaurant that was once a gas station for the trucks that carried cargo in and out of the warehouses. Now it's known for decent pizza and nachos and really good bluegrass music. Grady's been listening to the music and letting Gwen eat his nachos.

"Distracted," he answers Gwen.

She sips from a bottle of beer that she only ordered after he said it was fine. "You know you can tell me, right? If you aren't fine."

He nods and watches the banjo player. Nothing quite like a truly gifted banjo player, the kind who's been playing nearly his whole life, who learned from his daddy, who learned from his daddy—Grady pushes his nacho basket all the way over to Gwen. He's not hungry after all.

"Do you think I should do something? Or I should *want* to do something? I mean it's too late to go to his funeral."

Gwen lifts a chip weighed down by cheese and jalapeño peppers. "There's not really a rule book for this sort of thing." A slice of pepper plops back into the basket. "And you don't have to decide immediately, either. Not like he's going anywhere." She winces. "Shit, sorry. That was crass."

Grady shakes his head and one corner of his mouth lifts. "You? Crass? Never."

She laughs and jabs another loaded nacho chip dripping cheese and peppers in his direction. "Oh, fuck you, Grady. I'm trying to help here."

Grady's stomach unclenches a little. They eat and talk about lighter things, Cayo mostly, and some of Gwen's increasingly outlandish ideas for his bachelor party. The restaurant is dim, and their table is pretty private, but still he notices some people noticing him. They're left alone until their plates are cleared and they're arguing over who should pay.

"Grady?"

He turns to say he'll do one quick picture outside, when he sees a familiar face. "Spencer. Wow, I thought you were still in L.A.?"

"I was but I— Oh. Hi, Gwen." He gives a little wave.

"Hey, Spencer," Gwen says, unsurprised to see him and much friendlier than Grady would have expected, given how things went down among Gwen, Clementine, Flora, and Spencer when he spilled rumors to a tabloid, causing trouble for everyone involved. Nico isn't crazy about Spencer either, but Spencer was a good assistant to Grady and a good guy. Some people take longer to get their heads on straight is all. "I didn't know you were back here. Did you know?" he asks Gwen, though she clearly did.

"I extended an olive branch, because that's just the sort of kind and generous person that I am," Gwen says, swirling her beer bottle and burping. "I feel like Oprah."

"Oh, well. You look good, Spence. I'm glad you're back." He really is, and Spencer does look good in new glasses and with his hair in a less severely parted, trendier style. He's filled out some, seems more comfortable in his skin.

"Yeah I wanted to start over, I guess. Humble myself and try again." He gestures at his apron, black and covered with food stains with *The Pump Station* embroidered on it. "Doesn't get much lower than dishwasher."

"Doesn't it though?" Gwen cuts in.

Spencer takes a step back. "Right. Well, better get back to it." He holds up his dish bin and starts to turn away. "Good to see you, Gwen. And, Grady, I—" Whatever he was planning to say is drowned out by the sudden flurry of an electric fiddle solo, then he's gone, weaving through the tables back to the kitchen.

"That was weird," Grady says. "What's he all skittish about?"

Gwen takes a sip of beer and says, "Mm, well. Nico hates him, and you're with Nico so mathematically speaking, by the transitive property, that means you hate him. He thinks you're just going to write him off."

Grady cranes to see the kitchen; he can't see anything but steam and rubber floor mats. "I wouldn't do that. I wouldn't write anyone off."

Gwen, blunt as always, replies, "Wouldn't you, though?"

Grady's stomach roils with another wave of nausea. Gwen pats his hand and implores him to eat something, a milkshake at least.

He wonders if his mother knows yet.

6

He's never needed much sleep; drove his Memaw crazy
when he'd be up at five in the morning rarin' to go and bouncing
off the walls. It's not much different now. In the mornings, he gets
restless, excited by the sun rising on a new day, too much on his
mind to stay asleep, too much energy coursing through his body
to stay in bed. Nico, meanwhile, hoards sleep like an angry dragon,
and is just as mean if it gets interrupted.

Grady kisses the spikes of black hair sticking out from under
the blanket, pulls on underwear and running shorts, a tank top
and baseball cap, and sneakers. He cues up Tom Petty's "Runnin'
Down a Dream" on his running playlist, tucks his iPod into an
armband, and hits the dirt trail that snakes up behind their house
while the morning still shivers with dew. The trail connects with a
bigger trail that connects to a paved greenway that routes through
the woods all over Nashville. It's not quite acres and acres of his
own forested land, but it's a close enough compromise. As long as
he can get to the woods, where the creek runs companionably along

as he goes at a steady pace, out here where he can gulp lungfuls of fresh air and think about nothing but the pounding of his feet on the ground and Pink Floyd's "Run Like Hell" wailing in his ears, he doesn't mind the compromise.

Back at home, Nico sleeps on, while Grady struggles through eating one of those chalky protein bars Nico likes to pretend are real food, then uses their home gym to lift. The laundry is just off the steps leading from the workout room, so, after his workout, Grady peels his sweaty clothes off there. His overheated skin cools quickly in the air conditioning on his way to the third floor. When he was growing up, the shower in the trailer was an old dribbling thing. It had two temperatures: tepid and freezing. Grady blasts hot water through both shower heads and all of the jets, just because he can.

"Morning, gorgeous," Grady says, when Nico finally shuffles into the kitchen. Grady loves Nico when he's all done up: hair intentionally, painstakingly disheveled; his cheeks soft and fragrant from shaving; wearing an outfit so trendy even the fashion magazines can't keep up. But he loves Nico like this just as much: bleary-eyed and grunting and hair unintentionally messy. Nico sits at the breakfast bar and stares blankly into space. Creases from the pillow still mark one cheek, and his hair seems to be struggling to stay alert, too, as it flops into his face. Grady slides him a steaming cup of coffee.

"I was thinking we could head into town? And eat at this restaurant me and Gwen found before we go to the florist? If we leave soon we should have time. It's in an old gas station. I know that sounds weird; it's not. And there's a vintage vinyl store that opened recently across the street. How does that sound? Nice, right?"

Nico squeezes his eyes closed and takes sip after sip of coffee. "Too many words," he whispers, pained.

"Sorry," Grady whispers back. They don't often get a lot of Sundays with one only lonely item on their respective to-do lists. "Lunch. Record Store. Florist. Yes?"

Nico's eyes open again; they're a little less vacant. "Yes."

The lunch rush is in full swing by the time they get to The Pump Station; it's later than Grady hoped. The band is a Sunday-morning-appropriate, mellow acoustic ensemble: snare drum and hi-hat, guitar, upright bass, no singer. Once again, Grady forgets about the food and watches them play. He's also keeping an eye out for a certain someone who may be washing dishes.

"We have to decide on napkins for the reception," Nico says.

Grady turns away from the stage. "We do?"

"Well, yes," Nico cuts a bite off of the end of the veggie pizza. "People will need napkins, and they aren't going to magically a—"

"Oh, my gosh! You're Grady Dawson! Can we get a picture?" The table is suddenly swarmed by a group of teenage girls. "We love you! I saw you at Bridgestone; you were so good!" one of them says.

"Will you sign my shirt?" asks another. A third holds her phone out, ready to take a picture. The people at the tables around them abandon their own conversations to stare at their table and all of the excited activity surrounding them. Nico's entire body has gone rigid and closed off.

"I'd love to chat with you ladies and take some pictures after I eat. Hang tight, and I'll meet you outside in fifteen minutes, all right?" Grady conjures up his most beguiling grin. They scurry outside in a giggling, breathless huddle to wait for him.

He leans over the table to take Nico's hand. "You were saying?"

"I was talking about napkins." He shakes his head and adds, "which seems sort of silly now."

"It's not. No." Nothing about their wedding is silly, nothing. "What do we need to decide on? Colors? Size?"

Nico squeezes his hand, visibly trying to shake himself out of the fan-induced funk. He tries so hard for Grady, puts up with so much; it squeezes at Grady's chest and throat.

"Well, paper or fabric first of all. If we do paper, we can have something printed on them. *Nico and Grady: Happily Ever After.* Or something not terrible." Nico rolls his eyes at himself. Grady grins, he loves that, *happily ever after.* "Or with cloth, we can have them monogrammed with our initials, that's an option. Then we need to decide on size: cocktail, luncheon, dinner. A combination of all three? So maybe cloth for dinner, paper cocktail napkins for drinks; printing on both is too much, obviously…"

The people at the table directly behind Nico finish their meals and leave, and, as Nico keeps talking about napkins, Spencer arrives as Grady hoped he would, with his dishpan and dirty apron, to clear the table.

"Okay, so. Cloth for dinner," Grady says. "Paper for drinks. Sounds good to me." He's trying to focus on Nico and only Nico, but his gaze keeps slipping over Nico's head to Spencer.

"Great, okay. Making progress, look at us. So, now color. Have we decided on a color scheme or not?" Nico's head tilts. "What are you looking at?" Grady had a plan to reunite Nico and Spencer by having them run into each other very briefly. He wants Nico to see that Spencer is trying, that he's turned over a new leaf. Maybe they *can* trust him with a wedding invitation. Maybe Grady *wasn't* wrong about him.

Nico twists around in his chair before Grady gets a chance to put his plan into phase one. "Oh." He says, flatly, turning back around. "Him."

"Why, look who's here!" Grady says, complete with a flourish of both hands. "Spencer!"

At the sound of his name, Spencer's head whips up. "Oh, hey, guys."

Nico doesn't look at Spencer, only at Grady, his eyes narrow severely, and his jaw ticks left to right.

"So, Spencer works here now," Grady tries. Spencer comes closer.

"I gathered," Nico snaps. The air around the table is chilly; the band's easy-listening vibe sounds ironically sinister. Nico says nothing, Spencer shifts from one foot to the other. Grady shoves half a slice of pizza into his mouth.

"I'll go over... anywhere. Now." Spencer says, after several false starts where he mostly stutters. He goes back to clearing the table.

Nico goes back to talking about napkins, as if they hadn't been sidelined by seeing Spencer. "We can always just do white or black, that's easy enough, but there's still a matter of material: linen, cotton, polyester, a poly-cotton blend, a linen-cotton blend, a poly-linen blend." He lists all of the possible cloth napkin materials with unwavering eye contact, daring Grady to look away or lose focus. He doesn't. "Linen. Black. Or, oh. Dark green."

"Are you guys planning an event?" Spencer asks, loading the last of the dirty silverware. "I've been trying to get into event planning. I did my mom's second *and* third weddings to rave reviews. I'd love to help."

Nico says "No" at the exact moment that Grady says "Yes."

Grady leans over to plead his case, to gently nudge Nico into giving Spencer a chance; surely he can be trusted to order napkins?

Nico stops him with tap on his wrist, an invisible watch. "It's been fifteen minutes."

The girls are still outside, patiently standing by a car with someone's mom. Grady thanks her first—she's really just caught in the crosshairs—then turns his attention to the group. They're all very sweet, and one apologizes for interrupting his lunch.

"No worries, darlin'. I'm always happy to meet a fan. I appreciate your patience." He wouldn't be anywhere or anyone without them. Forget the record company and publicity agents and booking agents and his manager. These girls right here, they make it happen. He's more than happy to hug them and take pictures and sign their shirts and record a video for their friend Sadie who is going to "flip out," so they say. Grady waves as they drive off and walks back to the entrance, where he's accosted by Spencer.

"He hates me."

Grady rubs the back of his neck. "Well…"

"I messed up; I admit that. That's the first step, right?" Spencer rushes on, making chopping motions with his hands while he talks. "I wanted to be successful and in-demand and I thought I could just skip the hard work part and go right to the glamorous parts, and it's too late to fix it. I burned every bridge and now I'll be forced to wash dishes for the rest of my pathetic life." Spencer drops against the painted brick wall and groans.

Grady is sympathetic, that sort of regret and guilt is an all-too-familiar burden. It's also getting hot out, and he'd really like to finish his pizza. "I'm gonna let you in on a little secret. Nico can come across as harsh and judgmental." Spencer laughs a *no-shit* sort of laugh. Grady pushes on. "What most people don't know though, is that he's actually incredibly kind and understanding. Besides, if there's anyone who believes in a fresh start, it's Nico. He just needs to be sure that you really mean it."

Spencer looks skeptical, though he does push himself off the wall to stand. "You think he might forgive me? Do you? Give me another chance. I swear, I'll prove it you."

Grady nods and gives Spencer a squeeze on the shoulder as they go back and he heads to the kitchen. Grady is risking a lot. If their wedding goes public before it happens, Nico will be devastated. Can Grady take the chance of ruining this one day that will be theirs only—one day without fans and reporters and paparazzi and gossip, that's all Nico is asking of him? And Grady is putting that on the line for what? To help Spencer or to ignore his own problems?

The rest of lunch is quiet and interruption free, no fans or Spencer, and the music has gone quiet between sets. A final decision is made on the napkins: hunter green for the cloth and paper napkins, the cloth will be monogrammed in white.

"We should get going if you want time to browse at the record store," Nico says, checking the time on his phone. He missed a message. "My mom wants regular updates at the florist."

"Well, of course," Grady agrees.

And then, Spencer runs up, skidding to halt with his glasses falling off. "Wait! I got. Something." He pants and presses his side. "Ran home to get this. Probably fired now." He thunks a clear glass bottle full of pale brown liquid on the table. "I remember you buying these in L.A. once and bringing them back because you can't find it here. And when I saw it while I was there, I bought some because you were so excited about it. I admit I thought it was annoying and pretentious at first, and the taste takes some getting used to, but I'm hooked on it now. Anyway. Here. My last one." He puts his glasses on straight.

Nico turns the bottle to read the simple white label: *Los Angeles Booch.* "Kombucha. Can't get this brand here, and mango passion fruit flavor even, that's hard to find." He smiles at the bottle. Under the table, Grady gives Spencer a thumbs up.

"If you're busy today, I can help," Spencer says. "I heard something about a florist."

7

"I know what you're doing." Nico trails him down the row of pop country records and around the low, wooden shelf to a bluegrass display. That band at the restaurant has put Grady in a mood. Grady picks up a record, examines the front, flips it over, and reads the back.

"I'm sure I have no idea what you're talkin' about." Grady puts the record back and picks up the one behind it.

The record store is small and seems to skew to the obscure; there's an entire section of Norwegian Psytrance albums. Still, the bluegrass section is interesting, with authentic Appalachian mountain music, and the store has that comforting record store smell: musty and dusty with subtle notes of plastic wrap and patchouli oil. He picks up and puts down another record, stalling.

"Let's say we give him a chance, and he blabs to some tabloid that we're—" Nico glances around, there's barely anyone in the store. Still he bends close to whisper, "*getting married,*" as if the place is filled with tabloid spies.

"He never, ever broke my trust, Nico. Not once," Grady says as he pulls another record from the shelf. He'd even go so far as to say Spencer was loyal to a fault, putting his own job and reputation on the line to defend Grady. He was a little overbearing and inappropriate at times, yes, but the guy always meant well. "Come on," Grady says, dropping his voice low and running one finger along Nico's arm, up and down and up, while leaning into his space. "For me?" And to really bring it home, he drops his chin and blinks up at Nico through his eyelashes.

Goosebumps rise on Nico's skin when Grady draws his finger up his bicep again. "Oh for—Fine. If it means that much to you, *fine.*" Grady does a celebratory fist pump, and Nico jabs a finger in Grady's chest. "If this turns into a media storm and we have to get married in an underground bunker in Mexico, that is entirely on you, agreed?"

"Yes, sir." Grady says, serious.

Nico glances up to the ceiling, then relents with a sigh, "Well, go get him."

Outside, Nico clicks the key fob in his pocket that makes his Miata come to life with an excited *bleep-bloop* and flash of lights. Grady rushes back to the restaurant just in time to catch Spencer being chewed out by his manager for taking an unscheduled break.

"Bad time?" Grady says after the manager storms away.

Spencer punches his timecard and yanks off his apron. "My entire life is a bad time."

Maybe this little task will cheer him right up. Grady fills him in on the details and isn't sure if Spencer's dropped open mouth and bugged out eyes are from shock and horror or shock and excitement.

"Same phone number?" Nico asks as they approach; his hip is propped on the closed car door. Spencer nods, and Nico pulls out his phone. "I've talked to the florist on the phone. Today she's pulled samples," Never sparing Spencer even a moment of eye contact, Nico taps away at his phone. "You will consult with my mother as this is very important to her—I'm sending her number to you now: Amy, that's her—and all final decisions will be run past me and Grady."

"Got it." Spencer glances at his phone when it chimes with Nico's texts, then he clutches it under his chin.

Nico taps on his phone a little more, pockets it, and pushes off the car. "Let me be very clear." His spine lengthens, his shoulders square, his wide-legged stance is confident and intimidating. "If you so much as get a single hair out of line and speak to anyone about this, you will long for the days of being elbow deep in disgusting lukewarm dishwater. That is a promise. Do you understand me? Do not breathe a *word*."

Spencer nods like a wind-up toy. As Spencer rushes off to the florist, Nico calls after him, "Don't make me regret this!"

Grady adds, "Bye, Spence! Thanks for the help!"

After they get into the car and buckle up, Nico asks, "Didn't you want to buy something in the record store?"

Grady rubs his palms up and down his own thighs. "Yeah, but I need you to take me home now." His voice sounds strained to his own ears; he shifts in his seat.

Nico narrows his eyes, glances down. Then he looks away and starts the car. "I should probably be concerned by how much me yelling at people turns you on."

"We'll worry about that later," Grady says, shifting again. "Just drive fast."

Nico slides on his sunglasses, checks his mirror, and scoffs, "Please," before peeling out onto the street and gunning it. Telling

Nico to drive fast is like telling him to look fantastic; he's way ahead of everyone. By some miracle, they make it home and up the stairs, shedding clothes on the way, tripping onto their bed with mouths fused and Grady doing his level best to get them both all the way naked as quickly as possible.

"Inside me," Grady says, another unnecessary request as Nico's hard cock is slipping and pressing along his crack. He's heavy on top of Grady, kissing him with tongue and teeth and pinning Grady's hands above his head. Grady can't do much from this position, but the restriction makes him even hotter for it, and Nico knows that; it's no secret that he likes when Nico gets aggressive like this. The drive was agony for Grady and then made worse when Nico's hands strayed to Grady's lap at every red light and stop sign, then moved casually back to the gear shift, as if he wasn't trying to make Grady come in his Wrangler's in broad daylight.

Now, he does manage to get his legs free, crosses them over Nico's back, and presses his heels into the dip low on Nico's spine. Grady's pelvis tilts, and his cock rubs on Nico's belly.

"Okay, okay." Nico releases one of Grady's wrists to fumble lube out from a drawer in the side table. With his newly freed hand, Grady grips Nico's ass and grinds him down even harder, then takes advantage of Nico's fumbling with the bottle's cap and licks along the shell of his ear. A groan punches from Nico's chest, and he drops the lube. "Oh, my fucking—Give me a second, Grady, fuck."

Grady grins crookedly up at him. Payback is a bitch.

Finally Nico fingers him open, and he pushes in, slowly filling Grady with his thick, gorgeous cock. Grady puts his own hands over his head and crosses them at the wrist, and Nico quickly takes the hint, pins Grady's hands, and thrusts into him with long, slow rolls of his body.

"Lord almighty, *yes*." Grady moans. Nico snickers in his ear, and Grady does not care one single whit. It's perfect, then better than perfect, when Nico hikes up one of Grady thighs and switches to a quick, hard pace, hitting the spot that makes Grady sees stars. His orgasm starts to wind tightly in his gut, and he works his hand between their bodies to take himself right over the edge—

Nico's phone chimes with a text message. He stills.

"No, no," Grady says, trying to move himself on Nico's cock without much success. "Sweetheart, please." He's so close. So, so close.

"Shh, hold on." Nico reaches out to lift his phone off the table. "Hm. Do we want our boutonnieres to match?"

Grady's moan this time is one of extreme displeasure. "Who gives a shit? Keep going." He tries not to cuss too often. It's distasteful coming from his mouth, or so he was always told. But sometimes a *dang* or a *shoot* just doesn't quite cover it.

Nico clicks his tongue and props up on his hands. "This is our wedding, Grady." He sits up on his knees and slides out of Grady, almost all the way, until just the blunt tip is still inside him. Grady worries that he's upset Nico; of course he didn't mean that. Tensions are a little high at the moment; that's all. But Nico is smirking down at him and his eyes dance; he's winding him up again. "I give many shits, and so should you. Now. Will our boutonnieres match, or not?"

Grady takes a slow breath to clear his mind from the ache in his balls and the throb of his dick. Boutonnieres. Flowers. Pinned to their suits. Their suits won't match so... "Coordinating, not matching."

"Oh, good answer." Nico snaps his hips, picking up a new sharp rhythm. He wraps his hand around Grady's neglected cock and works him over in time with his thrusts. It doesn't take long for Grady to approach the edge again.

Nico's phone chimes.

"*No*," he means it to be stern; it's more of a whine.

Nico doesn't stop, though, doesn't slow his hips or the rapid movement of his wrist. His voice is strained now, wheezing out, "Rose petals?"

"No," Grady says again, so lust-addled he's not even sure what he's disagreeing with. He's gone, riding a crest of blissful release, coming down laughing and lax, letting Nico bend him over and pound into him until he finishes, too.

"Roses where?" Grady says when his sense return. He looks to his left, where Nico has flopped on his stomach.

"The aisle." Nico's eyes are closed; his mouth is tipped up into a very satisfied smile.

"Oh. Then, no." Too much. Nico hums a sound of agreement, and Grady takes advantage of the rare moment without layers of beautiful and expensive clothes covering Nico's body to draw his fingers down Nico's spine, across the muscles of his lower back in the inward bend, then over the firm rise of his ass. He smacks it, just because.

Nico yelps, flips over to glare at him, and, in the process, gives Grady an even better view. He may look angry, but his cock tells another story: twitching and plumping up. Grady dives in for a hard kiss. He's pretty confident about the probability of a round two when Nico's phone goes off, ringing instead of chiming a text.

"Seriously?" Grady says, as Nico sits up to retrieve it from the end of the bed. "Are flowers that difficult?"

Nico shrugs. "Hello?" He stands and turns to face Grady as he listens, which offers Grady the best view yet. If he moved forward just a little, Grady's mouth would be—

The phone hits Grady's hipbone. "It's for you," Nico says. "Vince."

Grady picks it up, trying to work out why Vince called Nico's phone and not his. Oh, he took his pants off on the first floor, and his phone is still in the front right pocket.

"Grady, finally. Thank god."

"Hey, Vince, what's up?" He sits with his legs over the edge of the mattress. Nico ruffles Grady's hair and heads to the bathroom.

Grady loses the thread of the conversation while Nico is walking away naked; he's too mesmerized by the lift and clench of his ass to think of anything else. He tunes back in just in time to hear Vince's panicked, "…have to tell them something. The label is breathing down my neck. Are you fixing the song or not?"

Fixing.

Grady's happy buzz evaporates, replaced by sick dread. "Oh," he says. "That."

8

He doesn't want to be difficult; he never has. He never wanted to be more of burden than he already was, because Memaw and Granddaddy were old and tired and doing so much for him as it was, but his mind and body would zip around and boil over with energy and anger and he didn't know how to stop it. He doesn't want to be difficult now, but music is where he channels boiling-over emotions and too much energy and too many thoughts. He doesn't know how to make music without grabbing it from deep in his soul with both hands and wrenching it out, bloody and alive. That's the secret: When he's asked in interviews how he makes music that seems so honest, it's because he doesn't know any other way.

For days he struggles with the song. He told Vince he would work on it, so he does. He spends hours in the practice room at home: during the day while Nico is at work, late night when Nico is sleeping, early in the morning when Nico is sleeping. No matter how he tries to rearrange and shift and rewrite, he can't make it something it isn't.

"Make it less personal," Vince advised, well-meaning. He's on Grady's side, bless him, truly. "Write it so anyone listening will believe it's about them." But it isn't about *anyone*.

> *And when I hold your hand*
> *O, lord, I understand*
> *What a man can do to a man.*

He's spinning circles on the drum stool in a corner when Nico calls to say he's running late. Grady has never been able to master the drums—too many things to coordinate. He keeps a five-piece kit just in case the band wants to drop by for a quick set. It's also nice to bang away at on occasion. He twirls a drumstick in one hand as Nico's exasperated voice comes through the phone speaker. "I'm swamped with shipments right now," Nico says, the strain in his voice clear over the phone speakers. "Clementine has been MIA so I took on some extra clients and— *shit*." Several somethings thump and thunder in the background. Just boxes falling, Grady hopes.

"Call Spencer, he'll help you." Grady taps at the edge of the high-hat. *Ting-ting-ta-ting.*

"Don't push your luck." Nico grunts with the effort of picking up something. "We'll have to drive straight to the bakery, so be ready. I'll let you know when I'm on my way."

Grady is only too eager for an excuse to pack it in for the day. "Will do," he says, complete with a drum roll and flourish. Grady changes out of his mud-spattered pants—he took an ATV break that didn't clear his head as much as he'd hoped—and into one of the outfits that Nico not-so-subtly placed in the front of his closet. The first is blue chambray slacks, a short-sleeved collared shirt, and brown suspenders.

He stands in front of the full-length mirror in Nico's closet. The shirt is slim-fit and snug on his chest and biceps. The pants fit just right: The waist is flat on his belly and the top ridge of his hipbones; the hem brushes the top of his feet without folding over. The soft fabric hugs his thighs, and, he cranes to see, his ass looks amazing, if he does say so himself. That man knows his stuff. Grady pulls the suspenders out with both thumbs hooked in the straps. It looks like something he'd have to do in a photoshoot: *Turn to the left. Chin down. Flex your arms. Look behind me. Click.* He releases the suspenders with a *snap* against his chest, then sits on the bed to lace up his boots.

Grady touches up his hair with a little anti-frizz cream. He watches some funny animal videos and sends his favorites to Clementine—he knows she loves them—and Nico still isn't home. He fishes in his knitting basket for his current project, but he needs more yarn. It's time to visit Nico's yarn-spinning friend in her funky yellow and purple house. He gives up and goes back to the studio to noodle around some more.

"Here you are. Are you ready?" Nico looks and sounds just as stressed out as he did on the phone.

"I thought you were gonna call," Grady shouts over the reverb of his wailing electric guitar. He snaps it off, and a jarring silence fills the space.

"I did." He pushes his hands through his hair, leaving the front standing up like a salute.

Grady frowns, puts the guitar in a stand, and retrieves his phone from on top of a bass amp. *Three missed calls: Nico.* "Oh." He must not have heard it. "Sor—"

Nico cuts off his apology with an impatient flutter of his hands. "It doesn't matter. We can still make it if we hurry." Nico leads them into the garage, then stops in the space between Grady's truck and his little red car. "You look nice, by the way," he says.

"So do you." Grady hooks two fingers in the gap between the last two buttons on Nico's shirt; it's dark blue with an oversized red rose print. "Paul Smith?" His pants are also red; his shoes are brushed tan suede. Brogues, Grady's pretty sure. He has a hard time telling brogues from oxfords.

"Very good. My car or yours?"

Grady tugs on his shirt. "Do I get a kiss for guessing right?"

Nico gives a little huff of impatience, but turns for a kiss that starts perfunctorily and quickly heats. Nico pulls back with his mouth still soft and his shoulders and spine relaxed just a bit. Grady reaches up to fix his hair, and Nico leans into his touch and sighs, "We have to go eat cake."

Grady pecks his mouth one more time. "Let's take the Belvedere."

"Feeling nostalgic?" Nico says, smoothing his shirt.

"Sorta." He had been thinking about his grandfather when he was puttering around the house with nothing to do. He'd given the Belvedere a polish and remembered the old pictures he would show Grady. He would set Grady on his knee in that worn out recliner of his, with its scratchy green upholstery that smelled like cigar smoke and always had a newspaper stuffed into the side. Grady has very few memories of his grandfather that don't feature that old recliner.

Back when cars were cars, he'd say in his voice that was like whisky: deep and rich and smoky, he'd call his car: *My best girl.* Memaw would tut, Granddaddy would rasp a laugh, and Grady would nod as if he knew. Granddaddy's car was a two-tone light blue V-6 sport coupe and Grady's is a cherry-red and white V-8 club sedan. Granddaddy sold his to buy an engagement ring and a down payment on a house for his new bride, and Grady bought his with his second big royalty check, after he'd wrecked the car he bought with his first one. He touches the faint scar on his bottom lip. He'd been lucky to walk away from a major wreck with only that, but at the time he'd wished he was a little less lucky.

On the way to the bakery, the rock-country station plays on the radio, the brand new air conditioning blasts—naturally his grandfather didn't have that in his *best girl* either—and Grady asks about Nico's day, he loves listening to Nico when he rambles on about his day; how animated he gets; how he's so excited to share it all with Grady.

He likes his new clients, Nico tells him; they're all nice enough and easy to work with. Then he goes on for a while about each of them, and Grady can tell he does enjoy working with them. Nico explains how it's just that he's gotten accustomed to having only one, and big star or no, it means less inventory. "And I know what Clementine wants now, what works. Easy." Nico flips the sunshade down; this time of the year the sun is still blazing low in the sky even as the clock claims it's evening.

"Are you unhappy doing it?" Grady asks. If he can figure out this song, get another hit, another big tour, Nico wouldn't have to work at all. Isn't it Grady's turn to take care of him?

"It's okay." Nico checks the map pulled up on his phone. "Next right. How about you? Were you working on something? I thought you were done."

It's his chance to tell Nico everything: How Duke wants to change the song and Vince is on his case, gently, but still; how he wants to make everyone happy, especially Nico, but how he can't do it without compromising his convictions; how conflicted he is and how, no matter what he does, he can't make the song be anything other than the truth of his heart. "I'm tinkering," he says. Then, "*Sweet Thang Bakery?*" Grady asks as a pink and green sign comes into view.

"It comes highly recommended, so we're just going to go ahead and ignore that name."

They're warmly greeted by two pale-haired women, one older and one younger, who turn out to be mother and daughter bakery owners, and they are both just as sweet as can be, even though he and Nico are a bit late and everything is rushed. The whole place smells like vanilla and buttercream and chocolate. Grady's stomach growls when they sit at the tasting table.

"This is my dinner," he confesses to Nico.

"*Grady,*" he chides, then flips a page in the laminated wedding cake binder and admits, "Mine too."

Grady sneaks a smiling kiss to his cheek.

"Okay, you two are adorable," the daughter says. Nico thanks her, and Grady sends her a wink. She blushes bright pink.

"Behave yourself," Nico says, then to the mother, "Could we start with the citrus cake with lemon curd filling and orange lemon icing?"

"What about a wedding pie?" Grady asks, taking note of a key lime pie in the display case that makes his mouth water. Nico sends him a sidelong glance with his mouth pinched. Well, regardless, that key lime pie is coming home with him tonight.

On the drive home they're too full of cake to talk about much of anything, and when they get home it's too late for Grady to do much more than deposit his pie in the fridge, take Nico to bed, and chase the taste of German chocolate cake and coconut pecan frosting from his tongue, while he sighs and whines and whispers Grady's name.

If Grady spends one more day cooped up in the house accomplishing nothing, he's liable to start climbing the walls. *Gone crazy as a bedbug*, Granddaddy used to say to him after too many rainy days stuck inside. He takes the Plymouth out for a drive.

He takes a highway west out of town and eventually drives down narrow country roads that cut through woods and farms and not much else. He's got the windows open, the radio loud, and his left arm draped out in the warm, rushing air. Out here, poor and forgotten towns spring up suddenly, like pockmarks on the otherwise clear horizon.

Grady's grandfather worked second shift as a chrome buffer at a tool manufacturing warehouse. He ground down rough edges before sending industrial tool parts off to the assembly line until he was too sickly to work, when Grady was eight or so. Until then, Grady had rarely seen his grandfather without a drink in his hand: a bourbon or whisky neat.

At five o'clock every evening they'd have happy hour, and Granddaddy would set Grady down in his old recliner and hand him cheese and peanut butter crackers while Memaw fixed dinner. With dinner, grandfather would have a Bloody Mary, until his doctor told him his liver was shot and he switched to plain tomato juice. It was too late to really make a difference.

Grady catches a whiff of a smell that he'd know anywhere as he comes around the sloping bend to another rough blue-collar town: barbecue. He follows the billowing smoke of the pit to a church: a single-room, white clapboard-sided building with a bell tower pitched high on the roof. Parishioners are gathered on the lawn balancing paper plates on one hand with their minds half on eating and half on gossiping; Grady knows that from experience.

He's strayed so far from Nashville that he's crossed over the imaginary barbecue line, from Nashville's spicy red-sauce doused ribs to a Memphis-style dry rub. Yet the table is covered with potato salad, cole slaw, deviled eggs, cornbread, and at the end, cobblers and pies and cookies and cakes exactly like the church picnics of Grady's childhood, as if he drove all this way to come back home.

He loads a plate so full of food the center bends in and the edges droop and if he closes his eyes he can imagine Memaw tucking a paper napkin into his collar and tutting at him to *try chewing for a change, land's sake, Grady.*

"Well, aren't you a big strong boy!" A plump gray-haired woman squeezes his arm. "Make sure you get seconds, you hear?"

"Yes, ma'am," Grady says, after swallowing a bite of cornbread and meat.

"Aren't you Elaine's grandson?" She lifts her pink-framed bifocals on a chain to get a better look at him.

"No, ma'am." He eats a deviled egg in one bite.

"Oh, I thought for sure I recognized you!" She flaps her hands over her face to lower her glasses and laughs. "Goodness, the older I get the more touched in the head I am!" Grady smiles at her, amused at being recognized—but not quite. She closely tracks the movement of his plastic fork across his plate; anticipation lights in her eyes whenever he goes near the potato salad.

"Well, I don't know about that, but whoever made this potato salad oughta be nominated for sainthood." He takes another bite, and *mm-mms* his way through chewing and swallowing.

"Oh!" She says, delighted, squeezing his arm again. "You know, it was really my mother's recipe. God rest her soul."

It is delicious, not exactly like Memaw's; she added horseradish, a touch of pickle brine, Duke's mayonnaise of course, and a secret something else that was buried when she was. Grady's never been able to replicate it. "My mistake then," Grady says. Her grip loosens. "Clearly this potato salad is the work of an angel."

Her name is Emma, and she brings him two plates of pie and cobbler and cookies and cake, then invites him to meet her granddaughter next Sunday after service.

"I'm afraid I'm already spoken for," Grady tells her. "Engaged."

But Emma's not upset; she brings him a plate covered in foil to take home to his betrothed. Church people, gotta love 'em. Grady dumps his trash and rubs his bloated belly and puts off worrying about the number of crunches and squats and miles of running he'll need to work that meal off, then he passes by an empty pickle jar with some change and a handful of dollar bills crumpled at the bottom. A label written on pink construction paper taped on the lid reads: *BBQ Fundraiser for Libertyville Presbyterian Food Pantry.*

Grady empties his wallet. It's only fifty-two dollars and twelve cents. Well, even podunk towns in the middle of Western Tennessee have ATMs. Grady jumps in his truck to backtrack up the road to where he spotted a bank before taking the church barbecue detour. He withdraws the max amount and when he circles around the bank's exit, it spits him out onto a different side street. That's when he spots it.

His feet carry him out of the truck and to the front door before he knows it's happening. He knocks on the front door of the brick house with knee-high weeds and a yard full of rusting cars. "The Plymouth," he says to the confused-looking man in the open doorway. "How much would you take for it?"

He's late for dinner, not that he's hungry—after the church picnic meal he could hibernate for the rest of summer—still he's anxious to get home after getting sidetracked and then sidetracked again. Nico is pretty easy going about meal times, generally. They both tend to eat when they remember to stop working for a second, but tonight is one of their potluck gatherings. Everyone is probably waiting on him. But, wanting to build the anticipation, he doesn't call until he's coming up their driveway. "Come outside, I have a surprise for you." He can hear the hum of several conversations in the background of Nico's phone.

"What surprise?"

"Nico," Grady scoffs. "I can't tell you. Then it won't be a surprise." So obstinate, that man, he *swears*. Grady pulls into the garage, dives out of his car, and ducks under the garage door as it rolls down. He practically skips up the stone walkway to the front door.

Nico is waiting on the bottom step. "Well?"

"Wait for it." Grady looks down the hill, trying to see through the cover of trees to the road. Nothing. Nothing. Nico's impatience is palpable, which just ratchets Grady's excitement up higher. Nothing...

"There!"

A tow truck rumbles up the drive, struggles with the steep incline and narrow driveway, but it makes it, eventually. It stops with a screech of brakes and shuddering engine. Wide-eyed and grinning like a fool, Grady spins to face Nico.

"Um," Nico says. "What am I looking at, exactly?"

The tow truck driver unhooks the heavy chains holding the car securely on the flatbed. Grady gestures to it as if he's Vanna frickin' White. "It's a 1970 Plymouth Superbird!" He dances closer to it, waving his arms even more emphatically as if Nico is unable to see an entire car on an enormous, loud tow truck sitting at the top of their driveway. "See?"

"Oh, I see all right." His flat expression remains unmoved.

"The guy wouldn't take any money, just gave it to me for free. He said his son left it there years ago and it's an eyesore. Can you believe that?"

Nico's expression does change; he arches one imperious eyebrow. "Yes. Yes, I can."

"Don't worry I'm gonna send some him money anyway."

"Yeah that's the part I was worried about," Nico deadpans.

He clearly doesn't get it. "You don't get it," Grady says, hopping from foot to foot while the platform lowers behind him with a shrill grinding noise. "They only made around two thousand of these! Richard Petty raced in one, and NASCAR banned it because it was too powerful!" Finally, the flatbed stops, and the car is free. Grady reaches in through the busted passenger side window for the most exciting part. He beeps the horn: *Meep-meep*. It's wheezy and weak after decaying in weeds for so long. But it's there, clear as day, that definitive roadrunner beep: *Meep-meep*.

"What do you think?" Grady asks. Nico can sometimes be hard to read.

"That depends," he says crossing his arms and giving the car a coolly assessing once-over. "Have you had a recent tetanus shot?"

So the car is a little rusty. Grady rests his hand on the hood; the spot disintegrates under his palm. He lifts his hand to brush off rust flecks. It's a lot rusty. And the tires are all flat. The windshield is cracked, and one side window is completely missing. The headlamps are the concealed pop-up style, and the left one has rusted-out hinges and has flapped permanently closed, giving the car a lazy-eyed sagging look. The interior is somehow even worse than the outside: the seats shredded, the floorboards and dash caked with dirt and grime.

After Grady signs the receipt and other paperwork and sends the tow truck rumbling away, he slings an arm over Nico's shoulders and frames the car with his hands. "Picture it," he starts, "Like the clients you had before working with the ever-glamourous Clementine Campbell. The ones who were a little rough around the edges—" Nico makes a skeptical noise in his throat after the words "a little rough;" Grady continues on. "Even when everyone else had written them off as hopeless and beyond repair, you found something in them. That shimmering pearl of who they were, hidden deep down in the slimy muck, and you brought it to the surface and made it shine." He stands in front of Nico and slides his other arm around him. "You saw who they really were and never gave up on them just because they had a few rusty patches."

Nico's face softens.

"I'm talkin' about me," Grady adds, just in case Nico needs clarification.

Nico laughs, knocks Grady arms away, and says, "I know that, dummy." Hands on his hips, he looks at the car again, shakes his head, and sighs. "Let's push it into the garage, then. It's supposed to storm, and that thing can't afford any more rusting."

Grady pushes the back of the car, under the absurdly high and incredibly cool back spoiler. Walking alongside the open driver's side door, Nico steers the car while Grady pushes, digging deep and pushing hard; the car is a monster. He decides not to mention that he also spent eight hundred fifty-two dollars and twelve cents on a church barbecue somewhere out in Western Tennessee. He'll explain later, over Nico's own plate of foil-covered church picnic delicacies, courtesy of someone else's Memaw. Grady beeps the horn again once it's safely parked and follows Nico inside to greet everyone.

The only person who greets Grady in return when he enters the dining room is Cayo in his clip-on highchair, who reaches for him with sticky hands and a stickier face. "Every time I see this boy, he's a mess," Grady says, tickling a clean spot on his belly.

Gwen scrapes more cut up pasta and fruit onto Cayo's plate. He picks up the pieces very studiously with his thumb and pointer finger, then mashes them against his mouth.

"Do you hear that, Bubba?" Gwen says, "Uncle Grady wants to clean you up after dinner!"

"Ha!" Flora says, reaching over to Gwen for high-five. Then she says more softly to Grady, "Hi, Grady. How have you been?"

It's clear from the concern in her eyes that she's gently prodding him about both his father and the issues with his song. Grady tosses her a grin and drops sideways into a chair. He shrugs. "Fine."

"Where did you go, anyway?" Nico asks from across the table.

"Yeah, and what did you decide to do?" Gwen asks. Nico tilts his head. Grady can't quite reach Gwen to kick her under the table.

He pretends he didn't hear either question. Looking around the table, he can see that they didn't wait for him after all. The serving dish of rotini pasta with red sauce and the wooden salad bowl are nearly empty; the bread plate has two dry crusts left. Even the cheesecake has been nearly decimated.

From his other side, Clem notices his assessment of the dinner spread. "Gotta get while the gettin's good, sugar."

"Speaking of getting," Grady replies, taking some cheesecake before it's too late. "How are things going with Ellis?" He's trying to shift the focus from himself, and it works: All heads swivel in Clem's direction.

"Wait. Who is Ellis?"

"Oh, are you dating? That's so wonderful, Clementine."

"Is that what you've been doing? Or *who* you've been doing, I guess."

Grady is close enough to Clementine to get a swift kick in the shin. She's wearing those sharp heels of hers; that's just cruel. Grady frowns and rubs his leg as Clementine is bombarded with more questions. When the doorbell rings, they all pause.

Gwen breaks the silence. "Is that her? Or him? Or them? Did you invite Ellis to dinner? Are you in love? Can I get all the dirty details now or later?"

Clementine calmly sips her wine and slides Gwen a look. "I'ma let you stew in all those questions for as long as possible."

Nico stands, laughing, and tosses his cloth napkin onto the table. "I'll get it."

Grady can't manage to eat more than half a slice of cheesecake, and the girls are still trading quips and pestering Clem with questions, so he follows Nico. He hopes it's not another certified letter bearing news that Grady doesn't know what do with.

"Spencer."

"Hey, Spence."

He looks like a shadow, small and dark and hesitating in a corner of the porch. Grady flips on the porch light, and he startles. "I—" There's a file folder in his hands. He holds it out to Nico and stands straighter after he hands it off. "I went through and called all of the ministers and officiants on the list. The ones who aren't available are crossed out. The ones I think you'd like best are highlighted. And one of them said he was a shaman who unites souls linked through time, so I went ahead and crossed him out, too."

"Good." Nico flaps the folder in a dismissive kind of way. "Night."

Nico turns back into the house, and, when he's out of sight, Grady says, "He's warming up to you."

"Oh, for sure. Any moment now we'll be planning a boys' weekend in Cabo." Spencer scowls. Finally, a genuine glimpse of Spencer's true self; Grady's thrilled to see it.

"Ah, he's all bark." Grady squints, remembering a few times when Nico has bitten, too. "Usually," Grady amends. "Why don't you come in for a spell?"

Spencer takes a step back, shaking his head. "Hard pass." He trots down the steps still scowling and falls back into shadows. "Have a good night, Grady. And thanks."

The potluck gathering moves outside to their patio, which is lit up in the mellow reds and oranges of paper lanterns hanging from trellises. Gwen hands Grady a marinara-sauce-coated Cayo, who wiggles and cries and tries to arch out of Grady's arms as Grady cleans him up. "What are you kickin' up such a fuss for?" Grady sets him down on the living room rug after he nearly does a backflip out of his arms. "Land's sake."

Cayo sits on the rug and cries, rubs his eyes, and droops to one side; must be near to bedtime, poor little guy. Grady's guitar is still stashed behind the couch from his last fruitless attempt to change the song. He pulls it out and sits cross-legged across from Cayo.

"Cay-Cay," Grady sings, strumming a slow chord. Cayo's cries fade, and he blinks his big brown eyes at Grady. "Memaw used to sing this to me when I was sad." He strums as he talks, and Cayo finally quiets completely. "I used to kick up a fuss a lot, too. Don't even worry about it." He plays the intro, and Cayo watches, then Grady sings to him, and Cayo bobs to the music. "There you go," Grady says. He picks up the tempo, and Cayo smiles, pushes up on unsteady legs, and totters closer. Memaw would sing this to Grady when he was sleepy, too, and still for once. She'd perch on his bed and run her hand through his curls. No matter how much grief Grady caused her during the day, she'd sing him to sleep—until he got too old for it and wished every night that he wasn't.

Flora quietly enters the room when the song is finished and Grady is letting Cayo grab at the guitar strings and pat a hollow non-beat on the body of it.

"He still hanging in there?"

Cayo looks up at her and rubs his eyes with balled-up fists.

"Barely," Grady says without needing to. She picks Cayo up, and he immediately tucks his face into her neck and curls his little body against her chest.

"We should probably head out."

"Yeah." Grady is surprised at how melancholy his voice sounds. Too much reminiscing, he supposes.

Flora runs her hand through Cayo's wild curls, then does the same to Grady's. "Come by this week for dinner."

Grady nods. "Yeah."

After everyone leaves and they finish cleaning up, Grady goes back to give the Superbird a closer look. He hasn't even glanced at the engine; it may be in worse shape than anything, which is really saying something. The hood opens with an unholy shriek, and, by the florescent lights in the garage, Grady discovers an engine just as busted up as the rest of the car, with dangling wires and missing parts to boot. The first thing he needs to do is get the car up on blocks and start yanking out the parts that will never work again.

The interior door to the garage opens. "Any rats nesting in there?" Nico says. He comes down the stairs and rests a hip on the car's grill.

Grady glances at the interior with its holes and pulled out stuffing. "Not at the moment."

They look silently into the engine. Grady tinkers; Nico's arms cross over his chest. "You've been kind of quiet tonight."

"Busy day. Guess I'm worn out." Grady twists a spark plug and yanks it from its terminal. When he brushes off the corrosion, he finds a melted electrode and an insulator that's turned white. He'll have to dig out his Granddaddy's old Chilton car repair manuals to double check what all that means, but he knows it isn't good.

Nico stands and stares at the engine while Grady yanks all the spark plugs and tosses them out, then bends over the engine to blow dust and corrosion from the empty holes left behind. "Do you think," Nico says when Grady is back upright. "That the car and Spencer might have something do with your dad?"

Grady gives him a quizzical look while he brushes off his hands. "Not really."

"I mean. Second chances. Repairing things." He reaches in to fiddle with a rusted out bolt, then pulls his hand away with a grimace. "Maybe if you talked about it—"

"Talk about what? Grieving a father that didn't want anything to do with me except to hit me up for money?" The world hasn't suffered any great loss at the death of Vaughn Dawson, and neither has Grady. Nothing has changed for him.

Nico steps closer, holding his rust and dirt covered hand awkwardly out to the side. "You can grieve that. I know you held out hope that he would change someday, and now he can't, and it's okay to be upset about that."

"Well, I'm not," Grady says brusquely.

"Grady, would you just—"

"I know you're trying to be helpful," Grady cuts in. "But I really need you to leave this alone. Please." The day has been too long already. He has too much time to think as it is; he doesn't need to drag anything else to the surface right now.

Nico obviously doesn't want to let it go; his mouth is tight, and his nose is flared. He nods, though, and says nothing more. Grady reaches for his dirty hand and brushes it off on his own T-shirt. "Thank you."

The doorbell rings again as they're going up the stairs to their room.

"Spencer again?" Grady wonders.

Nico backtracks down the stairs. "I haven't asked him to do anything else yet. That's pushy even for him." The house is dark. Even the outside lanterns are off; there's just the glow of the porch light to lead their way. "It better not be another fan who has no concept of boundaries. I will not be nice about them showing up at our house."

Grady is *pretty* sure Vince took care of the address leak. Still, he's worried when Nico opens the door. Grady doesn't like being stern with fans; he knows they mean well.

"I'm looking for Grady Dawson."

He knows that voice. He will always know that voice.

"Look, you can't just show up here," Nico says. Grady calls his name to stop him.

"It's trespassing."

"Nico."

"Grady has a right to privacy in his own home."

"*Nico*."

"This time I won't call the cops but—" He looks over his shoulder, the door only open as far at the chain lock will allow. "What?"

"That's not a fan. It's my mother."

11

In the room where no one ever sits, Grady stares out the picture window to the right of their stone fireplace as if he can see more than dark shapes standing out against darker shapes. Nico—who is truly Amy Takahashi's child in this moment—asks in the span of one breath if she is thirsty or hungry or has a place to stay and does she know there's a storm on the way because their driveway gets muddy and treacherous in the rain.

"Are you in town for long?" Nico continues.

"She never is," Grady tells the window.

"I'm… I'm out in Knoxville now," she says. "Staying with some family here."

"Family?" Nico perks up. "As in, also Grady's family?"

Nico's eyes on Grady are imploring, desperate for this to be something it isn't. Grady shifts, turning away. The couches in this room are too hard, and the new leather smell of them is too strong. He doesn't want to be here; he can't do this right now.

"Oh. Well, Vaughn's family. Clay? That's how I—" She knows then, about Vaughn and the wedding both, so either she's here to capitalize on his current vulnerabilities, or she doesn't care about having any tact at all anymore. The leather creaks as she shifts on the couch opposite theirs. "I apologize for showing up on your doorstep. I only had the address and I was gonna wait 'till tomorrow, but I was so anxious I figured I'd go ahead and get it over with. I can go."

Grady finally looks at her, really looks. He's not sure how long it's been. He stopped counting the days of her absences a long time ago. Two years? Three? She doesn't look much different. Her hair is shorter. "You should go," he tells her flatly.

Nico slaps his hands on his legs and stands. "I would really like some tea right now. Everyone want tea? Yes. Grady, help me *make tea* in the kitchen, would you?" Nico purses his lips and darts his eyes to the kitchen and back, silently transmitting his displeasure in a not-at-all subtle way. Well, that makes two of them. Grady glowers all the way to the kitchen.

"What are you doing?" Nico fills the tea kettle with the kitchen faucet on full blast. "I have never seen you act so rudely. I didn't know you even had that capability."

"What can I say? My mother brings out the best in me." When he was a kid, and she would come and then go, Grady would be a hellion for days. He doesn't know how his grandparents put up with him. He sighs and scrubs his hands through his hair; Nico shouldn't have to put up with it either. He tries to be more diplomatic as Nico clangs the top of the kettle closed. "She's gonna put on the charm," Grady says. "Act like she's really gotten her life together, for real this time, ask for money *just to get her on her feet,* and then take off again."

Nico places the tea kettle on the stove and turns on the burner. "She seemed genuinely happy to see you."

"Yeah, she's good at that."

"Still. I get to meet your mom, that's something." He mutters, fussing around the kitchen to gather mugs and tea, a serving tray, and a squeeze bottle of honey. "You don't look very much alike."

With her heart-shaped face, small nose, and pointed chin, she looks quite a bit like Memaw. Granddaddy is there in the narrow slope of her shoulders, her hazel eyes, and the shape of her mouth, particularly when she's sad.

"I look like my father," Grady says. He shakes tea into a diffuser. "Looked."

"See? I didn't know that. And now I do." Nico's smile is optimistic in the face of Grady's pessimism; it's an interesting new dynamic for them.

"This is not gonna to end well, sweetheart. I don't want you to get your hopes up here." Grady helps prepare the tea, trying to be more cooperative now that he's wrapped his head around his mother showing up out of the blue. He snaps one diffuser ball closed and drops it into a mug. The tea blend is something Amy sent; it has lavender petals in it, and when Nico pours the steaming water over it it smells like flowers and lemons.

"Tea. That's it. Then we can toss her out by the scruff of her neck." Nico presses his hands flat together in the center of his chest, as if pleading with Grady—as if Grady would ever deny him anything.

Nico and his mother get along like two peas in a pod, naturally. They first bond over the tea and then how much she loves their house: "It's fancy, but not like Elvis fancy." Bonding continues over Nico's career, and how she could use a good stylist, and then

Nico is giving her tips and complimenting her shape and how she clearly has an eye for patterns. Grady's calming tea is completely ineffective.

"So, Lily. What are you up to in Knoxville?"

"Oh, it's Lillian. No one has called me Lily in a quite a while." She blinks as if remembering something difficult.

"Harder for people to track you down if you change your name, right?" Grady says, setting his mug back in the wooden serving tray.

"Grady…" Nico smiles with his teeth clenched tight.

"I mean it's true, right, *Lillian*? You owe someone money. Or you screwed them over. Made promises you never intended on keeping and skipped town. Don't want to make it too easy." Grady's right eye ticks twice.

Silence stretches out until Lillian scowls down into her empty mug, and Nico says, "Oh. Yeah, now I see the resemblance."

Grady can't take another second; he's heard enough. "I'll be in the garage. Nico'll write a check for however much you came here for."

He yanks out wires and belts and starts unscrewing bolts, not knowing or caring what works still. He hates this. He hates the anger he can't control; he hates that it still gets to him, *she* still gets to him. After all he's accomplished, all he's done, the life he's built for himself without her, without *anyone*, goes sideways and upside down the second she comes breezing back into his life. He's a stupid little boy again, waiting for his mama to come back for him.

"She left." Nico approaches him as if he's made of broken glass; staying a safe distance back, he inches his way across the cement floor.

"Good." Grady cranks the handle of a ratchet wrench, trying to loosen a stubborn bolt.

"I think maybe you should hear her out."

"It's not worth it. Trust me." The car shakes with his efforts, and still the dammed bolt refuses to budge. "It's the same thing every time with her."

Nico hesitates, coming closer and then moving back again. His voice is so soft, so hesitant, so unlike him; it's not right, not Nico. "Your father is gone, Grady. She's not. You can still have a relationship with her, you know. You could try."

Wrench in hand, Grady moves to face him—as if he hasn't tried, as if that isn't exactly what he's wanted his *whole life*. "For once, Nico, can you let something go when I ask you to let it go?" He's too loud, he's shouting. It sounds so cold and hollow, and he hates it; god, he *hates* this.

Nico has never been one to cower, and, just like that, the gentleness is gone, replaced with a sudden snap of anger. *Good.* "Sorry for fucking caring about you, Grady. What is with you tonight? Why are you shutting me out when all I want to do is help?"

"Stop. Helping." He goes back to that goddamn bolt, pushing and pushing. And the more stubborn it is, the more anger spreads like acid in Grady's belly. "Stop acting like you always know what's best for me. Stop going behind my back and doing things I asked you not to do. Stop treating me like your client or your child or some idiot who can't even figure out how to dress himself in the morning." Grady growls a curse at the goddamn stuck bolt. "I was doing just fine before you came along. Just fine."

Nico doesn't shout back. He's very quiet, says nothing when he leaves, and closes the door whisper-soft. That makes Grady even angrier; he doesn't get to just *walk away*, not again—

Then Nico's absence is a sudden vacuum, as if all the air in the room and in Grady's lungs has been sucked out. He could scream and act out with his grandparents because he knew they were safe, that they weren't leaving. No matter how awful he was they would be there—until they weren't. Now Nico is his safe space, which means Nico has signed up for more than he bargained for.

12

The bed in the guest room is too soft. It's not firm-soft like their bed in the master bedroom: comfortable yet supportive. It's squishy-soft, as if Grady is being slowly swallowed whole by a giant man-eating dandelion fluff. He can't get comfortable, turning and shifting and curling, then uncurling. When he does finally get comfortable, he's too hot. Then, after he violently kicks the covers onto the floor, he's too cold. Grady never sleeps well when one or both of them is crisscrossing the globe for tours and press: Grady on his own and Nico with Clem and occasionally someone else. Being ten feet down the hall from the closed door of their bedroom, where, he hopes, Nico is getting a much better night's sleep, is so much worse than being across an ocean from him. He's too embarrassed to face him, to share a bed with the shame of Grady's outburst heavy between them, so Grady tosses and turns and sleeps in fitful, frustrating bursts.

Nico is up early and gone the next morning—no note, no breakfast or outfit laid out for Grady. This is what they do; they hurt each other and then run to the farthest corners they can find to lick their wounds alone. It was a necessity for Grady before, when he was the only person there to pick himself up and dust himself off, and he forgets; he acts on instinct, and it's only after that he remembers he's not alone anymore.

While he's stretching his calves for a run, he texts Clem: *Meet me at stairs,* and takes the paved greenway path that leads to that park. She's there when he arrives soaked in sweat and panting. Her hair is in a cute messy bun, and she's wearing designer workout gear and pink sneakers, as glam as always. Clementine Campbell knows to be photo-ready at all times. "My mother's back in town," Grady tells her. They jog up and down opposite sides of the wide cement staircase built into a hill.

"Yikes," Clem hits the bottom, then pivots to run back up. "You okay?"

Grady runs up the steps two at a time, keeping pace with Clementine. She's been on this merry-go-round with him before. Though he's never wanted to trouble her with it, she does at least know what it looks like. "No, not really."

At the top, they pause, pivoting to go down the staircase. "I know what you need," she says, pulling her phone out of a hidden pocket in her compression pants. She slows on the stairs, but doesn't stop, and Grady's phone buzzes in his armband. He stops on the third step from the bottom to watch a video of two otters holding hands while they float down a river.

"Thanks, Clem." Grady presses play again.

"I got your back, sugar."

Grady grins and sends her another text. *Be my best woman?*

"Duh," she yells, running back up the stairs.

After they finish, someone snaps a picture of them doing cool-down stretches. Grady can see the headline plastered over his sweaty red face: *Grady Dawson Struggles to Breathe! Is it drugs again? Lover's quarrel with a jilted Clementine?*

Clementine still looks perfect.

He runs back home; his head is clearer, and his body is flushed with endorphins. He steps out again, showered and shaved and nicely dressed, feeling hopeful, a little, as if maybe he's shaken off all of the frustration and anger and embarrassment, or maybe he's just found somewhere to shovel it aside. He stops by that organic farm-to-table sandwich shop Flora likes.

"I brought lunch."

Flora is on summer break, home full-time for a few months with Cayo for just a little longer now. "Oh, you are my favorite." She kisses his cheek and steps aside to let him in. Cayo dives for Grady's arms. "I was just trying to get him settled for a nap, give me... fifteen minutes."

Grady hefts Cayo's weight into his right arm. "I'll take him."

She blinks at him, and Grady notes how her usually neat braid is coming loose, with tufts of hair pulled out in random places down the length of it. There are at least three mystery stains on her shirt, and, he notes, unsure if it would be rude to point it out, a Cheerio is stuck in her cleavage.

"You are a life-saver. I was starting to think there was no world outside of toddler music class and Sesame Street and cleaning up Cheerios from literally *everywhere*." She shakes her head, and Grady decides to pluck out the Cheerio for her, since she sorta did mention it. From Grady's arms, Cayo reaches for it, and she smiles. "This is a very strange game you silly boy." Flora kisses Cayo and strokes his hair before taking the proffered bags of food.

In the wooden rocking chair next to a window, Grady softly sings a lullaby until Cayo's body goes limp and heavy against his chest, the tiny fist grasping Grady's sleeve relaxes, and his back rises and falls in slow, even breaths.

"You must be the luckiest little boy in the whole world," Grady says, placing him carefully in his crib. "*Two* mamas who'd do anything for you." He gives Flora a little more time to sit down and eat in peace, he tidies up the toys littering the bedroom floor, rights the books on their shelves, then tiptoes out.

"Are you staying for a while? We can sit outside." Flora is placing a sandwich in a container, for Gwen, Grady figures.

"I had some other stops to make," Grady says, as the friendlier of their two cats rubs against his leg. Crackers. He stoops over to pet her. "My mom is in town."

The cat hops up onto the kitchen counter. Flora nudges her back down. "Is that hard for you?"

Grady stays crouched on the floor even though Crackers has wandered off to the living room. "It is. She comes in with all these promises, and I should know better by now, but—"

"She's your mom," Flora fills in, her voice kind. "You want to believe her. I can understand that."

"You don't think I'm stupid," Grady says, standing. "For getting my hopes up every time?"

"Grady." Flora sets her hand on his arm in a gesture that is comfortingly maternal. "Not at all, no."

"Hey, Flora," Grady says, holding her hands in his and looking deep into her eyes. "Would you be my best woman at the wedding?" He leaves with hug and sealed *yes!* and a promise to return for dinner soon and a book Flora thinks he'll like and a finger-painted masterpiece by Cayo: a large sheet of paper covered nearly corner to corner in thick smears of blue paint, with a little yellow handprint mashed on the bottom. Flora says she has a drawer full of them, because, of course, that boy's favorite thing to do is make a mess. Grady's gonna frame it and hang it on the wall.

At his next stop, Grady stands in front of the bakery below the Style Studio as if he can't recall what he's doing there, but really he just can't pluck up the nerve to go to him. In the end, he skips to his last planned stop and walks around the corner to see Spencer at The Station Pump.

"I hear your so-called mother is in town." Spencer sloshes water from a pitcher into his glass. Has he been promoted to water-pourer? Is that a promotion? "How did you hear about that?" Someone in the park overheard, maybe? Great, more fuel to the gossip fire.

"I helped Gwen and Nico pack up some boxes and ship them." Spencer moves the dripping pitcher away from Grady's table.

"Oh. Well, that's promising."

Spencer scowls and cocks his hip sharply. "He said I was already on the payroll, so it was slightly less annoying than the hassle of hiring someone new."

"Ah." Grady bites down on a smile. That's his Nico. Spencer moves on to spill water at other tables, and Grady scans the menu. The hour is odd, early afternoon between the lunch and dinner rushes, and the restaurant is quiet. Just a handful of tables are filled, and no band is on stage.

"When's the live music starting?" Grady asks the waitress after ordering a salad and a soda; gotta balance things out.

"There should be one on now, but they had to cancel." She takes his menu. "Anything else I can get you in the meantime?"

Grady shakes his head. He stares at the stage. It never has been just the music that felt like a gravitational pull; music and stage were what he knew he was meant for, even when he fought it. He fights it now, turns away and unwraps his silverware from its paper napkin, puts the napkin on his lap, then smooths it out. He arranges the salt and pepper and hot sauce and ketchup in order, smallest to biggest, then biggest to smallest, then least favorite to most favorite. With the song and the album on hold, he doesn't know when he'll be on a stage. Maybe everything will be on hold, and the thought makes his brain and body twitch and tremble, as though the jumping, loud static is taking over again.

"You want to be up there so bad," Spencer says, making Grady startle. He sets down his drink and a straw. Maybe Spencer's new job is just *Drink Boy*. "You're practically vibrating out of your skin over here, and this is only your first Mello Yello."

"Nah." Grady leans back in his chair, casual-like, sipping the drink and wishing his attention would stop drifting to the empty stage. Spencer rolls his eyes.

The stage here reminds him of the stages he played on before anyone knew his name and no record label put demands and pressure on him. It was just him, a guitar, and a platform. He'd get payment in the form of drinks or food or games of pool. Sometimes people listened and sometimes not, and that didn't matter much to him. He had a stage and a song, and that was where he found his salvation.

"You think someone here has a guitar I can borrow?"

Spencer snorts. "Honey, this is Nashville."

A found guitar and cued-up spotlight later, Grady slides onto a stool, taps the mic, and launches into the first chords. He plays the song that's been confounding him for weeks now, but he doesn't try to change it, not a note or word or rhythm. He plays it the way it came to him: the lyrics he scribbled down on an airline napkin, hunched over a tray table on a plane ride home to Nico. This is the music that filled his head, chasing anything else away—doubts and worry and what ifs—so everything slotted into place just right; the song landed somewhere between major and minor, celebration and melancholy.

This song is the one he wants to release, not a song about anyone, a song about him, about finding a home and a love and a wholeness. With Nico. *Him.*

When Grady starts the chorus, Nico appears, stock still by the hostess stand, as if by magic. Grady falters, then recovers by shutting out the small gathered crowd, the staff, even what he's doing on stage; his eyes are only for Nico.

Once in a life, a boy comes along
And blows your world apart
With a love that burns so bright
It shines the light
Through the cracks of your broken heart.

The small crowd of patrons gives him a standing ovation, clapping and whistling with a few phones held up taking pictures and video. Grady bows and thanks them, is held up by photo and autograph requests, and Nico is gone when Grady manages to make it to the front of the restaurant. He leaves money with Spencer to pay for the meal he never ate and a nice tip for the waitress.

At Nico and Gwen's office building, he takes the stairs instead of the elevator; he can't stand still. Gwen is at her desk when he bangs open the door. "Hello, Grady," she says, as if she was expecting him to burst in exactly as he did.

"Where's Nico?"

She looks over, though her fingers continue to fly across her keyboard. "Spencer called him, and he took off out of here like his ass was on fire. I haven't a clue where."

"He came looking for me. I lost him. He didn't say anything?" Grady puts his hands on his hips. Where could he have gone? Is he even more upset now? Grady needs to apologize and he needs to tell Nico about the meeting with Duke and how he has to change that song, but he *can't*, and he wants to just let bygones be bygones with his mother and his father and move on, but he *can't*.

"No, sorry. He's been moody as hell all morning. I mean worse than usual." She looks back at her computer screen and pulls a face, then jams the backspace button on her keyboard several times with end of her pen.

"We got into a fight." Grady says.

"Christ, you two are exhausting." She throws her pen at him. "Well, what are you standing there for? Go find him!"

Nico doesn't have a collection of places he likes to tool around in town the way Grady does. When Grady's stressed out, he needs to move; when Nico is stressed out he needs to hunker down for a spell. Other than work and places connected to work, Gwen and Flora's house, and his car, Nico's sacred safe space is home. Grady checks a few boutiques and vintage stores and also the yarn spinner with the chickens wandering her yard, because Grady needs yarn anyway. Nico's not at any of them; he should have figured. When he gets home, Gwen sends him a message: *He's back at the office now and snippy. I'm going home. Exhausting, seriously.*

Grady yanks rusty bolts and dead wires from the Superbird, plays guitar for a while, and goes to bed alone again.

13

Before, when he got attached to every wrong person at the wrong time, when everyone pegged him as a fast and loose heartbreaker—and maybe he was, if breaking his own heart counts—Grady's most persistent fantasy was waking up in the morning and walking into a kitchen filled with sunshine and warmth and someone waiting for him at the stove. His partner: Someone who would stay, someone who saw all of him and all of his life and decided he wasn't too much, he was just right. It didn't seem like a lot to ask, but all the same, it was. For a long time, it was.

"You're here," Grady says. The morning is overcast, and Nico is sitting at the breakfast bar with a full cup of coffee and a half-full carafe. He's here and he's waiting for Grady.

"I do live here," Nico replies in a clipped tone. His eyes flit to Grady's; they're sad, not angry. He pours more black coffee into his mug. "We have venues to see today."

"Oh. Yeah." Grady goes to the fridge, and its constant-cool temperature is warmer than the air between them. "When did you get home last night?"

"Late."

Annoyed at the non-response, Grady slams the fridge door closed. "You sure you want to go look at wedding venues?" He asks, not without some bite. This is how they're planning the rest of their lives together? If this isn't what Nico really wants, then Grady isn't gonna force him, as though he's an obligation Nico has to meet. Grady sits across the breakfast bar from him and cracks open a soda. Nico's expression pinches.

"Please tell me that's not what you're having for breakfast."

"You're having what—Two? Three? Cups of coffee? How is that better?" He takes a swig of the Mello Yello and swallows with a loud gulp.

"Coffee has actual documented health benefits." He jerks his chin up to indicate the soda Grady is chugging. "Unlike that toxic waste. My god, at least eat some eggs or something."

His tone softens at the end in concern Nico can't quite disguise; the fretting and fussing over his health and happiness come from love. Grady goes back to the fridge and exchanges the soda for hard-boiled eggs and fruit. Nico nods his approval, then steals half the food, and they eat at the counter, as it starts to drizzle outside.

"And yes, I do really want to go see wedding venues still." Nico says it to the last dregs of his third cup of coffee, but his tone is gentle and his eyes are warm.

They've automatically ruled out any venue in which Grady has performed. "My wedding and home are the only places I get an escape from your career," Nico said, with the stiff body language that made it clear there was no arguing: spine straight, jaw set, chin tipped up.

"Fine, but no mansions, either," Grady countered. "Too hoity-toity." Nico mocked him for saying *hoity-toity*, but he agreed.

They drive to the first appointment with only the radio filling the quiet, then walk on either side of the event coordinator as she sells them on the features of the historic farmstead. There's a nice green garden for the ceremony, an old carriage house for the reception, and a large flat lawn for pictures. "We can set up horseshoes or bocce," the coordinator says, leading them across the lawn. "Croquet. Cornhole."

Nico makes a sour face, and Grady chokes out a little laugh. They finish the tour and leave with a packet of details and pricing that Nico slides into a binder marked *venues*. "Cornhole," he says as he starts the car. "Honestly."

They tour a church, which is nice enough, then a bed and breakfast outside of town, and a banquet hall downtown after that. With every stop, they talk a little more; the usual ease of their relationship is returning bit by bit. At a rooftop venue overlooking the neon lights of Lower Broadway, Nico presses his shoulder to Grady's.

"Not a bad view," he says, scanning the city below.

Grady looks at him: the sharp lines of his face in profile, long, lean torso bent over the balcony, dark eyes darting curiously. Grady can tell his mind is moving a thousand miles a second, taking everything in, and making smart, snap decisions.

"It is."

Nico gives Grady a wry look. He reaches for Grady's wrist and commands. "Come here."

"Yes, sir," Grady says, dropping his voice and his chin and moving in for a kiss. When their lips touch, it's like releasing a long-held breath. They still have things to talk about and issues to work through, but Grady knows they will.

"The song was perfect," Nico says, brushing his knuckles down the front of Grady's shirt. "If that's what you've been tinkering with, I think you got it."

Grady catches his hand when it comes to rest against Grady's stomach. "About that," Grady says, then the close-by click of heels on the rooftop patio interrupts him.

"You guys are a sweet couple," says the event manager, Kacey. "Would you like to see the area available for a sit-down dinner reception?"

"We would, yes," Nico says, following her, then waiting for Grady to fall into step beside him. "We also need you to sign a nondisclosure form, for—" He nods at Grady, and the manager doesn't miss a beat.

"Of course."

On the elevator down, Grady slumps against the wall and closes his eyes. "I like this one."

"Are you just saying that so we can be finished already?"

Grady crooks a grin and cracks one eye open. "Only a little."

Nico laughs, then rubs at his face and the back of his neck; he's tired, too. "Just one more. I know you hate this stuff."

Grady frowns, opens both eyes, and pushes off the wall. The elevator slows to a stop on the bottom floor. "I don't. I don't hate it. I just want to go ahead and get to the part where we're married."

Nico gives him one of those looks where he can't seem to work out if Grady is some baffling figment of his imagination, then smiles and says, "You're very sweet." Grady winks at him. The elevator doors slide open, they step off together, and all hell breaks loose.

"Grady! Grady! Over here!" Twenty people with cameras flashing strobe lights push and shove to get to the front of the mob. "Grady, can you make a statement? Nico! Over here! Are the rumors true?"

Grady shields his eyes and steps back; he needs a moment to get his bearings and— Nico. The paparazzi usually leave him alone in Nashville. Why are they yelling for him? Grady moves to get Nico back on the elevator so he can deal with the pushy gang of paparazzi himself, but the doors have closed.

"Nico, is it true this is all a publicity stunt?"

"I—What?" Nico rears back, groping the wall for the elevator button.

"When's the wedding?"

"Are you already married?"

"Can you make a statement about the marriage?"

"Has Grady really been dropped from his label?"

"Grady, over here!"

"Nico! Nico!"

"Look over here!"

Nico looks panicked and shocked and about as mad as a nest of hornets, as Grady's granddaddy would say. The elevator still hasn't come, so Grady has no choice but to make a statement to dampen the flames.

"Hey, all right. If there's anything to announce, you'll know when we announce it." He forces a winning smile, chats with some of the photographers he's familiar with, poses gamely, and ignores any other shouted questions and the relentless flash of cameras. The elevator arrives just after a security guard shows up to kick the paparazzi out.

"They know. Everyone knows." Nico is pressed tight into a corner of the elevator with his arms crossed protectively over his chest and his shoulders high and tight.

"I don't know how," Grady mutters, much less shaken than Nico, but dismayed all the same. All their fantasies of a private, intimate wedding have turned to smoke and gone, just like that.

"Someone leaked it, obviously," Nico snaps.

"Well, I didn't. Don't get pissed off at me." Grady, fuming, turns to face the doors.

"I'm not—I'm just—" Grady can hear his sigh and the whoosh of his hands raking through his hair. "I'm not blaming you."

Grady crosses his arms. "Sure as hell sounds like it."

They return to the rooftop, where Kacey greets them with an apology and an assurance that the paparazzi are being dispersed and they will be personally escorted from the building and that, of course, she had no idea they were down there.

"Do you want to just go home?" Grady asks, as they wait on the romantic rooftop deck that they can't possibly use for the wedding now. "Or if you'd rather go to your office alone…" Nico looks as if he'd like to bolt right over the edge of the roof; he's pacing and tugging at his bottom lip and messing his hair so much it's starting to look like his sex hair.

"No," he says, still short and brusque. "We have an appointment; may as well keep it."

Leaving Nico to pace behind him, Grady leans over the balcony and can't decide if he'd rather hit the fast forward button so they're already married, or the rewind button so they can start all over again. In any event, neither of them wanted the present situation to be this way.

14

"**I'm remembering why** we put this one at the bottom of the list," Nico mutters, cringing when the car hits another deep pothole in the gravel road. Time has come to a frustrating, grinding halt as they've crept and crept up this hillside thick with trees and, so far, nothing else at all. Nico grits his teeth and tries to speed up; the tires spin and the car fishtails.

"Shoulda driven my truck," Grady says. He's not looking at Nico, but Grady can sense the tense shift of his body, can almost hear his jaw grinding.

"You want to do this right now?"

He doesn't. He doesn't want to fight now or ever, and the truth is he's not angry with Nico. He feels guilty for putting him in this situation; he should have done more to protect him and protect their wedding and their privacy.

Finally, they reach a sign. Due to the shadowed dusk of the woods and heavy cloud cover, only when they're right up on it can they make out the letters burned into the wood: *Serenity Lodge.* They park at a rustic round building built on stilts, and Nico gets out to fuss over his tires and shocks and the dirt coating his formerly pristine paint job.

"Not a soul would be able to get up here without us knowing," Grady muses. Nico stops brushing dirt off the fender and looks around; the surly look on his face fades for the first time since the paparazzi debacle.

"That's true."

At the bottom of the split-wood staircase leading up to the lodge, the owner, Linden, introduces himself and gestures at a narrow space between the trees behind them. He has a soft, high voice, a narrow face, and a willowy build; he strikes Grady as a gentle forest sprite leading them to a magic portal hidden in the trees.

"I created this space for those who, by choice or necessity, are doing things differently," Linden says in his musical voice, as they approach a grassy clearing. "The idea is that your wedding day is yours, free from the turmoil of other's judgments or expectations." He gestures at the rustic ceremonial area: two rows of natural-cut wooden benches with a leaf-strewn path between and a simple arch made of branches at the end of the aisle. "Ensuring a peaceful ceremony that will lead to a peaceful marriage."

"If only," Nico says faintly. The fight is gone from him; he just sounds wistful and sad, and it's like a knife twisting in Grady's heart.

A phone trills from Linden's pocket. "Excuse me for just a moment."

Nico wanders down the aisle, then back, brushes a stray leaf from a bench. "It's pretty barebones, but it is isolated." He releases a long breath and looks up. "And peaceful."

Grady doesn't know how to fix this. He can't just snap his fingers and make the press and the fans and the tours and the demands of his record company disappear. He can't make his mother better; he couldn't make his father better. He has no buttons to push to move forward or back or rewrite what's been already been written. But he will make a promise to love, honor, and cherish Nico; he will do everything in his power to make Nico happy.

"Picture it," Grady starts, walking backward down the center aisle. "It's late fall, no more heat or humidity or afternoon rain." Nico tips his head at Grady as he gestures at the tree branches above him. "We'll hang origami cranes from the branches. Didn't you say something about that? Cranes?"

Nico's arms uncross and fall open. "I did."

"And we can string ropes with paper lanterns all across here," Grady continues, sweeping his arms over the space above the benches. There's a large, flat rock to the right of the tree-branch wedding altar. "We can set the band here. Or a harp?"

Nico nods, slowly making his way down the aisle. Grady's throat tightens. "A band," Nico says. "Just acoustic guitars."

He's playing along, and Grady is reinvigorated. "Yes. And we can decorate this with flowers, maybe?"

"Vines," Nico counters. "I like the symbolism: strength, perseverance. The cranes mean commitment and longevity."

It's not the tedium of wedding planning or the boredom of the seemingly pointless minutia that makes Grady want to skip ahead to the *I do's;* it's how overwhelmingly and completely he loves this man and wants to commit his life to him—all of it: good and bad, ups and downs, sickness and health. His life is a lot, *he* is a lot, yet somehow he found Nico who is still here, pinning down the details of their happily ever after, despite everything.

"We can come in at the same time from either side," Grady says, once Nico has joined him on the raised platform beneath the arch.

He clears his throat to loosen the sudden thickness in his voice. "And we'll say the vows that we wrote ourselves—"

"Oh, no, are we doing that?" Nico interrupts, spinning on his heel. "You write songs! That's not fair; yours will be so much better than mine." Nico clicks his tongue and flashes a hint of a smile.

"Yeah, they will," Grady teases back. "Not a dry eye in the house, guaranteed." He exaggerates his accent on the last word, hillbilly-style. Nico laughs, and Grady takes his hands.

"It'll be something like: Have you ever had a moment when you looked at someone and the whole world disappeared?" Hamming it up, he glances at the imaginary audience, then turns more seriously to Nico. "Even though we were on a red carpet in Hollywood with cameras and superstars—and their entourages and egos—" Nico laughs, but Grady doesn't. "Even with all that craziness, all I saw was you. And I knew I had to meet you. And then after I met you, I knew I had to get to know you more. And after I got to know you, I knew I had to kiss you. And after I kissed you—" He pauses again, not for effect, but to cope with the swell of emotion in his chest. "After I kissed you, I knew that I had to find some way to keep kissing you for the rest of my life."

Nico's eyes shine. "Grady…"

"It was you. All along, I had been looking for you in all the wrong places, trying to find your face in all the wrong people. I can't believe I found you. I can't believe I get to keep you. And I can't believe that I'm finally here, getting to marry you."

Nico releases Grady's hands to swipe quickly at his eyes. "See? How am I supposed to follow that?"

Grady smiles and winks. "I have an idea." He bends forward, and Nico cups his face, sweeping his thumbs over Grady's jaw.

"I love you. So much. I want to keep you, too." Nico whispers, closing his eyes.

Grady kisses him, soft, tender—serene. "That's all I need to hear."

Linden finds them at the altar still, bent together quietly. He waits until they untangle themselves. "I can show you the reception area now, if you'd like."

Grady glances at Nico, who dips his head in silent communication. This is the place; it's intimate, private, beautiful. No one in the world can bother them here. No one can take away the moment when they'll make a promise witnessed by family and friends and god and the universe and the trees to keep each other, for good.

"We'd like to go ahead and put down a deposit."

Halfway back down the hillside, they leave behind the peace of the forest and the dead-zone of no Wi-Fi or cell service. As soon as they cross the line back into the real world, their phones blow up with missed calls and voicemails, text messages and notifications. Grady pulls his phone from his pocket to see that the newest text on the screen is from Spencer: *IT WASN'T ME.*

"Can we just—" Nico's hands flex on the steering wheel. "That was so nice, out there. Can we just ignore the rest of the world for a little longer?"

Grady switches off his phone, then shuts it in the glove compartment for good measure. "Absolutely we can."

The ride back seems shorter than the drive in, easier, until they approach their street and both hold their breath until they can see that their driveway is free from press or photographers. Once safely inside the house, their only remaining sanctuary, the world disappears again. There is only Nico's mouth, and Nico's hands, and Nico's warm skin beneath his fingertips. They stumble up the stairs, but then, instead of turning left to their bedroom, Nico detaches his lips from Grady's and steps to the right. "Just one quick thing." He points to the green binder tucked beneath his arm.

Grady watches him disappear into the office and considers—he can go to their room and get a head start on the fun or they can just move the fun elsewhere. He follows Nico.

"Need to transfer the venue info from the planning binder to the official wedding binder…" Nico spins the chair around and pulls a blue binder from the top of the desk. Grady pivots the chair to the side, pushes Nico's legs wide, and goes to his knees.

"Grady." Nico looks down, blinking rapidly. "This really will only take a minute."

"Okay, go on then." Grady hums, runs his palms up the firm, long muscles of Nico's thighs, and adds, "I ain't stoppin' you."

Nico licks his lips, takes a shaky breath, and flips open his binders without moving the chair, and his lap, out of Grady's reach. The wedding binder has tabs and zippered pockets and color-coded lists. Nico flips sections until he finds the one he was looking for, and Grady slides his hands higher to tease at the soft bulge of Nico's balls. Nico's breath catches briefly, then Grady hears the snap of the binder's rings opening. He tugs the button of Nico's pants loose and pulls the zipper down. As Nico stretches to grab something else, Grady pulls Nico's soft cock from his briefs.

"Grady," Nico says, shaky and breathy and not nearly as chastising as he means it.

Grady drags his open mouth along the shaft; it swells as he goes. He looks up at Nico without pausing. "Uh-huh?"

"I'm…" Nico starts to explain, looking from Grady to his task, and seeming to lose the thread of whatever sentence he was trying to utter. He's struggling to slide a stack of paper into a three-hole punch; his hands fumble to get the paper into the tiny slot. Grady lifts his head, pauses deliberately, and Nico slips in the paper and slams down the hole punch. "Okay."

Grady sucks the head of Nico's cock between his lips, then moves down as he hardens against Grady's tongue, until he can hold him deep at the back of his fluttering throat. He loves this, loves being overwhelmed like this, focused only on the taste and feel of Nico filling his mouth and throat, fighting the urge to pull away by breathing slowly through his nose. It's only when Nico yanks on his hair and curses that Grady pulls slowly back.

"Fuck, Grady." Nico has either abandoned the wedding binder or finished with it, because his attention is no longer divided; he looks, heavy-lidded, at Grady, as his cock slips free from Grady's lips and stands fully hard and thick and flushed dark.

"Mm, there we go." Grady wraps his hand around the length and pumps a few times. "Look at you. Gorgeous." Nico's cock pulses in Grady's hand. Grady bends to suck him down again, but he only manages a few slow bobs of his head before Nico is pulling at his hair again.

"Shit—" He's panting and trembling and gasps out, "too fast, stand up." So Grady stands, and strips his shirt off as Nico takes care of Grady's jeans while still sitting in the chair. Then he kisses across Grady's pecs where the tattoos are inked. He works one of Grady's nipples with his teeth and tongue; liquid desire zaps down Grady's spine.

Two restless nights alone have made Grady hungry for Nico's touch, and now that his mouth and hands are all over him, licking and kissing his chest and stomach, hands greedy on Grady's ass and cock, Grady gives in to it completely, gluts himself on it, runs his fingers through Nico's glossy hair, and tips over the edge without realizing he was that close. He perches on the edge of the roll-top desk to catch his breath. "Sorry," he says, wincing at Nico's careful removal of his very nice, and now very soiled, shirt.

"Are you really?" Nico replies wryly, setting the shirt to the side; bare torso-ed and rock-hard, he leans back in the chair with his legs spread and eyebrows lifted.

"Nope," Grady answers, dropping back to his knees to finish what he started. Truth be told, he's not sorry about that at all.

15

"Thank you all for joining us today—" Nico rises, gesturing regally with a wide sweep of his arms to the group formed around the round table.

"You're welcome. This is my house, so I had no choice."

"Gwen."

"Any*way*," Nico sends a look to Gwen, then a nicer one to Flora, who is sitting next to her at the big round table in Gwen and Flora's dining area. "As I'm sure you've all heard by now, the news of our upcoming nuptials has, most unfortunately, been leaked to the media—"

"Does he think this a press conference?" Gwen stage-whispers to Clementine on Flora's other side. Clem is typing on her phone, but gives a little one-shouldered shrug. Spencer is next to Clementine, taking notes on a legal pad, and Grady is next to him. Grady suggested that maybe they should have a press conference, or an interview or magazine feature. Now that the barn door is open and the cows long gone, the easiest thing would be to go ahead and invite everyone inside. But Nico is convinced that they can still keep everything but the fact of the wedding's existence a secret, and Grady does enjoy watching his clever mind in scheming mode.

"Before we really begin, was anyone followed or possibly bugged before coming here today?" He glances suspiciously around the table as little Cayo toddles into the room, bringing a toy from the living room that he holds up for Gwen.

"Nico, chill. It's not like the mafia is out to get you." Gwen takes a toy phone with light-up buttons from Cayo and pretends to receive a phone call. "Hello? Oh hi! It's for you, Bubba!" Cayo takes the phone and toddles back to the living room. "No one was bugged."

"They're worse than the mafia," Nico retorts. "A relentless, privacy invading scourge."

"He ain't wrong," Clementine comments, still more focused on her phone than on Nico.

"Is anyone hungry?" Flora says. "I made cookies."

Everyone mumbles a "yes" or "yeah" or "sure."

"I need to repeat that I had nothing to do with this," Spencer says, again. "I learned my lesson. I didn't breathe a word, I sw—"

"We know!" Everyone else replies at the same time.

"Actually, yes, about that. Spencer, thank you." Nico says, and Spencer's mouth hangs open. "First order of business: Gwen can you track down who *did* leak it?"

"Oh, it was the bakery. Uh, Sweetie Yums or Sugar Buns or something equally as godawful. They posted a picture on Instagram of the type of cake you picked out."

"Sweet Thang," Grady supplies. Cayo appears at his side, offering a little wooden car with a peg person sitting in the driver's seat.

"Why thank you, kind sir," he tells Cayo, who gives him a drooling, four-toothed smile.

"Well, you really should have had *Sweet Buns* sign an NDA."

"I did," Nico snaps, "I think I did… We were so rushed, I don't… Shit, did we? And it's Sweet *Thang*— Ugh, why am I defending them?" Nico presses his thumb between his eyes the way he does when he's getting a tension headache. Grady spins the wheels on the tiny car and tags in to the discussion. "Everyone we've met with has signed a nondisclosure agreement. I remember."

"So, you gonna sue?" Gwen wonders.

"Ah, well," Grady rubs his chin and looks sheepishly down at the table. "My usual lawyer, uh, has declined to continue representing me." At least that's what Grady assumes, since he called Boomer Jenks this morning for advice about the situation—and his record company troubles, though Nico doesn't yet know about that—and Boomer said he'd "sooner tussle with a hungry grizzly bear than piss off Stomp Records" and advised Grady to find someone else. He'd really liked Boomer, too.

"That's unfortunate," Flora says.

Grady shrugs. "It's not the first time."

"That's because you pick these small-time lawyers who are happy to take your money," Nico interjects, "Then drop you instead of doing their jobs."

"I don't want some slick, big-city lawyer," Grady responds. "Like I'm some full-of-myself hotshot with a hotshot lawyer."

Spencer coos at Grady with mock sympathy, just like the old snarky Spencer that Grady knows and loves. "Aw. Isn't he precious? *Not* full of himself." Gwen snorts at that, and Flora, pressing a hand to her mouth, apologizes even as she laughs.

"Thanks, y'all." Grady says with a chuckle. Well, at least they keep him humble.

"Sugar," Clementine says, eyes still trained on her phone's screen. "You aren't playing dive bars in Shelbyville anymore. You need a hotshot lawyer. I got someone perfect for you; don't you worry."

Nico holds up a hand. "We aren't suing her. But we will take that lawyer."

After scrolling his phone, Spencer informs them, "She says in a comment that she did not tag either of you and did not know that you or anyone else could find it," He scrolls farther, adjusts his glasses, and looks up. "She does seem to feel bad."

"An unintentional shit-storm is still a shit-storm," Nico says through gritted teeth.

Spencer leans back, defensive. "I am just the messenger." Cayo strolls by and drops a stuffed bunny in Spencer's lap; he looks at it as if he has no idea what to do with such a thing.

"I'm aware, I'm—" Nico pinches the bridge of his nose, takes a deep breath, and releases it to say, "I know."

Grady fiddles with the toy car and frowns; Nico is getting upset just talking to their friends about what happened and how he wants to move forward, and Grady is becoming less and less confident that he can give Nico his private, peaceful wedding in the woods.

"Spencer." Nico tries again after several more meditative breaths; his tone is more even now. "If you could handle the rest of any in-person or over-the-phone meetings to finalize the wedding details, that would be very helpful. Put reservations under your name, or your mother's name. Hell, tell them it's for your dog's wedding for all I care, just as long as it doesn't have any connection whatsoever to me or Grady on paper or otherwise."

Spencer scribbles on his legal pad, then opens his phone to click rapidly on the screen. "Got it. Send whatever you need to me, and I can even link our calendars…"

As Spencer slips into work mode, Grady beams, glad to know that Spencer is coming through the way Grady hoped— *knew* he would. Flora brings cookies from the kitchen and Cayo abandons his toy-sharing to climb in her lap and demand a cookie.

"They're sugar-free banana flaxseed," Flora says. She hands Cayo one. "Sorry."

Nico takes one, but doesn't eat it, just uses it to gesture to Clementine. "Clem. Clem? *Clementine*." Grady sends his car zooming across the table. It lands in Clem's lap, and she finally looks up from her phone.

"Just a sec, hon. Trying to scramble and get some studio space." She swipes and types and sends off messages, then sets the phone down in front of her. "Apologies, go on."

"I don't suppose you have any ideas for how to get the heat off of us for a while?" Nico puts the cookie down and brushes crumbs from his fingers. "Any scandals you've been cooking up recently?"

"Sorry, sugar. I'm out of the scandal business these days." She casts a chagrined look at Gwen, then Flora. "But I'll see if I can come up with something else. Not like they're hard to distract, that lot."

Nico presses his hands flat in front of him, nods his head, and sits. "Well, that was all I had on my agenda. Grady?"

Grady shrugs. "That's it I guess." He takes a bite of the sugar-free banana, something-seed cookie. Not bad, actually. His Memaw made the most incredible homemade banana bread and these cookies are—well, also banana. And not bad.

"Hey, I have a thought," Flora says, helping Cayo climb down to the floor so he can go back to his toys. "I don't know if you're comfortable with this, Grady, but you said your mom is in town?"

Grady chews slowly. "Yes."

"I bet if the press were aware of that, if she'd be willing to give some interviews or… I don't really know how all that works, but I'd have to imagine that's a more interesting story than a wedding somewhere on the horizon and all they know about is the cake."

The cookie is dry and tough going down. "I don't know, Flora."

She looks away, cheeks pink. "That's fine, I understand why. I guess I was thinking, if nothing else, she can say whatever she came here to say, and you get to keep a safe emotional distance. And if it gets the press off your backs a little, maybe a win-win-win?"

Grady exchanges a thoughtful glance with Nico. Clem and Spencer are working away on their phones, and Gwen pipes up with, "My wife. Smart and pretty." Cayo wanders in and gives Grady a plastic toy tambourine, then grunts to be picked up, and Grady bounces him on his knee.

"It's totally up to you," Nico tells Grady. "Whatever you want."

Grady wishes he hadn't been so insistent on making decisions himself instead of letting Nico decide his life for him. He doesn't know what he wants. He doesn't know what she wants. His chest is tight, like a steel cage around his lungs.

As they leave Gwen and Flora's house later that evening, fireflies flicker across the yard. Nico comments on them; he always does, because they don't have fireflies in California. Nico used to say they didn't have fireflies "at home," but it's been a while since he's spoken of Nashville as a place where he's stuck for Grady's sake. Still, sometimes the guilt of Nico sacrificing so much for him lingers anyway. Hoping the stick shift and sporty engine will keep his mind occupied, Grady drives Nico's car. By the time they reach home, the stars have shimmered on to join the fireflies.

He stopped catching fireflies in jars when he was seven, or somewhere around there, whenever he became old enough to realize that they'd end up dead in the morning, no matter how many holes he punched in the lid or how many leaves and sticks he dropped in to keep them happy. Of course, an old jelly jar with a twig and a leaf isn't a substitute for the great wide open, but for a long time he thought it was his fault alone, as if he was a curse or menace, as if he was rotten somewhere he couldn't see. He had to be.

Look at *them* he was made up of *them*.

It makes him melancholy even now to see the fireflies light up in the summertime when he remembers that incredible, fleeting light that he wanted to keep for a little bit.

"We can just as easily lay low for a while," Nico says as they turn off a main road to the darker, slower side streets. "The gossip mill is brutal, but at least it's fast, like hives, or a bout of explosive diarrhea."

Grady glances over when they reach a stoplight. "It's just that my mama's kind of a loose cannon. I don't know if I can trust her to even read some simple canned statement that Vince cooks up." He looks back to the road when the light changes. The closer they get to their house, the more far apart and hidden behind rows of trees the houses become.

"Okay, then it's a nonstarter. We'll come up with something else. Whatever you want."

Grady drums his fingers on the steering wheel and guides the car down the isolated winding road that leads to their isolated winding driveway. Nico is opinionated; he's pushy and honest and decisive, and Grady loves that about him, even when it irritates him. This "whatever you want, dear" approach isn't right; it's as if Nico finally reached his breaking point and— broke.

"Right, but what do you—" Grady slows the car just before it reaches their driveway.

"Oh, hell," Nico fills in.

There are cars and people and cameras outside their house, and once they spot Nico's car, the mayhem begins: lights flash in a constant barrage, they can hear muffled yelling through the windows, and Grady has to creep the car through the crowd to avoid plowing the lot of them down. Some of the photographers approach the vehicle, bang on the hood and the roof, and snap picture after picture through the windows. Grady makes it past the property line, then guns it up the driveway. After one look at Nico's shaken, shocked face he decides: "I'll talk to her."

16

Southwest of Nashville's county line, the city development drops off quicker than elsewhere. It might be the geography: the undulating hills, dense forest, and meandering river, or maybe folks out here have had the same way of life so long they just don't take kindly to things changing too quickly. Grady grew up with Nashville looming large and just out of reach. If you ask him where he's from he'll say, "outside Nashville," but this is something else entirely: gently sloping hills and farmland and the low, slow river delta. Way on out here, they could be a million miles from home.

"Would it help if I got out and pushed? Does that car have a lawnmower engine? Come *on!*" Nico reaches over to honk the horn, even though Grady is driving; Grady catches his hand and folds their fingers together. "Settle down."

"Twenty miles under the speed limit, Grady!"

He looks downright mutinous, gesturing angrily with his free hand, pitched forward in his seat. Grady kisses his knuckles and smiles with his lips still pressed there. "The pace of life is a little slower out here, sweetheart." Nico flops against his seat and *humphs*.

Out here is the sort of place where people give directions like, "turn right just past the big cross, not the little one before that, the big one over near the Winn Dixie, then left at that rusty tractor there; if you go through the traffic light, you've gone on too far." Grady knows Clay's house by address only; he's sent money, through Vince, and never did bother to pay a visit.

"I've never seen this many trailer homes in a ten-mile stretch," Nico comments, checking the map on his phone. "What do people do out here? Oh, last turn up ahead." Grady has some idea, but he leaves it unsaid, just squeezes Nico's hand, takes the turn onto a gravel road, and Nico says, "I'm more anxious than you are. How are you so calm right now?"

Grady tips his head and grins in Nico's direction. "Practice," he says.

They pass a farmhouse, then pastures and rows of soybeans starting to wilt in the lingering summer sun. A clutch of houses and a couple of outbuildings appear, then an old gray plank-frame home that's half collapsed, long ago abandoned. After that, a few more little houses dot the gravel road. They stop at a small brick house that has a work shed out back nearly the same size as the house itself. Grady knocks, and there is no response or sign of life from inside. The place is small and old, but tidily kept with a trimmed yard and bushes, and everything on the house seems to be in good repair. A scraggly black cat perches on a workbench where power tools are tucked away.

"So this is your dad's brother or uncle?" Nico asks while they wait on the porch. He tugs at his tie and yanks loose the top button on his collar. It's a scorcher today. The calendar may be close to flipping over to fall, but the weather stubbornly refuses to follow along.

"His uncle," Grady says. He thinks he hears some shuffling inside the house. "If Vaughn had a brother, I don't know about him." Grady knows about Uncle Clay because he was the only person left in Vaughn's life who wasn't completely fed up with bailing him out of jail or paying off his debts or letting him sleep on their couch knowing he was bound to make off with something valuable. Grady sent him money and never came out here because—because they never came for him, did they?

The door opens to an older man with thin white hair and blue eyes much like Grady's own. He's tall and thin but for a round potbelly. His skin is the leathery brown achieved from years of days spent in the sun, and his hands are big and liver-spotted and rough-hewn. He looks at Grady, looks at Nico, and says, "All right," and turns back into the house, leaving the door open for them.

Nico sits ramrod straight on the edge of the couch with his hands pressed flat between his knees. Grady drops down next to him. Clay is in a diagonal corner, sitting in a well-used armchair. They sit for several minutes that seem longer, barely speaking beyond brief niceties. The inside is much the same as the outside of the house: aged, worn, but neat and well-maintained. It's cooler, though. Somewhere along the line, someone got fed up enough to install central air in this old house—thank the lord for small mercies.

"So… Did Lillian say when she'd be back? When I called she gave the impression that she was planning on being here?" Nico blurts after too much silence.

"Said she was goin' to the store. S'all I know." Clay's accent is so thick—Western Tennessee thick—that even Grady struggles to catch every word. Nico's face seems to indicate that he's caught very few. "Thought you'd bring your wife."

Nico's eyebrows shoot up in alarm; he caught that. Grady hesitates; they always do outside of the relatively safe bubble of progressive, artsy Nashville. He has no shame about coming from a poor rural area not all that different from this one, but that doesn't mean he's unaware of its problems. Grady thinks of the conversation with Duke at the record company, how his love song about a man is "controversial," that speaking honestly about his own self is "too political." Sometimes even the bubble isn't safe.

"No. Nico is my fiancé." Grady isn't ashamed of that either; he doesn't care what Duke or Clay or any small-minded so-called "fans" might have to say about it.

Clay stares at the two of them, clearly processing this information, and Nico sits up, somehow even more uncomfortably rigid. "All right," Clay says, then, "I have his stuff for you." He stands with difficulty, using the chair to push himself up and grimacing in pain, and then he lumbers to a room down the short hallway. He walks as if he has bum knees or a bad hip. When Clay returns, he deposits a large shoebox on Grady's lap. The picture of tan work boots on the front exactly matches the pair Clay is wearing.

"I don't want it," Grady says. "Thank you."

Clay grunts as he sits. "I'ma throw it away otherwise. May as well take it."

Grady looks at the box with his hands held over it as if he's afraid to touch it. He doesn't know what to do with it, or how to feel about it, but he doesn't want to burden Clay with it either. "All right," Grady says. Clay nods, and they go back to sitting in the small living room saying nothing, until Nico's phone vibrates in his pocket. He reads the message. His face twitches before he forces it to something more neutral. He shows it to Grady.

Lillian: Something came up. So sorry, can't make it.

It's exactly like her: unreliable, untrustworthy, full of shit. "I tried to tell you," he says, not wanting to be right. "She always does this." Nico just frowns.

They stand and thank Clay for his time and hospitality, and Clay congratulates them on the marriage that has yet to take place. When Nico asks to use the restroom before they make the drive back and disappears down the small hallway, Grady has to ask. "Is it your knees or hips?"

Clay's age- and work-worn hands drift to his legs. "Knees. Need 'em replaced. I work for myself, you know. Handyman stuff. Harder with bad knees. I manage all right."

"I'm sure." Grady laughs at himself. He tucks the shoebox under one arm; the contents shift and clatter. "You know I never did get the hang of that kinda thing. Could use a little work around the house if you're available."

"All right."

Grady shifts the box. "And why don't you schedule that replacement in the meantime and let me look at the bills."

Clay looks up at him, and it must be all Nico's talk of family and joining together that Grady does feel a kinship to Clay without really knowing him at all. What other blood relation does he have? "Don't have to do that," Clay answers.

"I know I don't. You took Vaughn in, though, so consider it a debt still owed."

Clay nods, then stares at him, scanning Grady's face as if he sees something he can't understand there. "You look like him, you know."

Nico returns from the bathroom and announces he's ready to go. "So I've heard," Grady replies.

He's relieved, more than anything, after they drive away. She did exactly what Grady expected her to, and now he doesn't have to have any guilt over not giving her a chance to say whatever she wanted to say: She had it, and she flaked out on him once again. Nico seems upset about it, though, picking at the cardboard lid of the box and flexing his jaw too hard.

Grady turns the radio up and starts singing along, and Nico smiles at him. He taps at the box and asks, "Can I?"

Grady shrugs. "Knock yourself out." It's the pointless flotsam and jetsam of a man he never knew; it's not as though he has any attachment to it. Still, he can't seem to bring himself to look while Nico gently picks through the items.

"Huh," Nico says, pulling something out. "There's a car key. And… an impound notice."

"Of course."

"It's in this town; can't be far." Nico dangles the key in the air. "Maybe we should take care of it while we're here?"

Grady would rather let the thing rust away to nothing, but if he doesn't pay the impound fees and get rid of it, then certainly they're going to come looking for Clay. "Yeah, okay," Grady says, and U-turns back toward town.

Forty-five minutes and an impound fee, towing fee, and six months of storage fees later, Grady is the proud owner of a gold-colored sedan with a broken transmission and cracked windshield that Vaughn, to Grady's entire lack of surprise, left abandoned on the side of the road. He pays yet another fee to have it towed to a mechanic near their house.

"You don't want to fix that one up?" Nico asks when they step back outside.

"There's hardly room for the cars that work in our garage," Grady says, walking back down the little downtown block to where they parked after they couldn't find a space near the impound lot. It's so hot and muggy out his shirt is sticking to his skin and Nico's hair is wilted and flat, not that Grady would be dumb enough to tell him that.

They were parked in front of a building partly covered with thick kudzu—looks as if it's been empty for a while now. This whole town seems to be filled with things that have been forgotten and left behind. Grady starts the engine to blast the air and give it a chance to cool before they get in, while Nico wanders to a large window that hasn't been overtaken by vines. "What do you guess this place was?"

Grady looks around. It's freestanding, just around the corner from the main street's antique shops and second-hand stores and mom-and-pop restaurants. This building is not huge, but it's bigger than the other stores here. A *For Sale* sign, faded and tipping to the side, is stuck on the window. "Pawn shop?"

Nico cups his hands on the window and peers between them. "Oh, maybe. No, I think it was a music store. Look."

The air coming from the truck's vents is cool now, and Grady would really like to get home and take his sweaty clothes off. He ducks over to see whatever it is Nico is seeing anyway. When his eyes adjust to the dark inside, he can make out a laminate-topped counter and industrial carpeting, what looks like a soundproof booth in a corner—the kind music stores have for testing out drum kits without giving all the other patrons pounding headaches—some hooks on the walls like the kind used for displaying guitars or fiddles or banjos. "Yeah, looks like it. Too bad, kids in this town could use a music store." Lord knows music saved his sorry ass in a place like this. "Come on, let's get the hell out of here."

17

The shoebox of Vaughn's things stays in the garage until Grady can decide what to do with it, and, in the meantime, the paparazzi become a permanent fixture lying in wait at the end of their property line to shout and take pictures and video every time Nico and Grady, separately or together, appear. Nico becomes resigned, choosing his outfit in the morning knowing full well it will appear on the tabloid sites, in magazines, and be smeared across social media. "If I'm going to be stalked and harassed," he says, "I'll look damn good while it's happening." Nico's determined resignation breaks Grady's heart.

The paparazzi are fewer early in the mornings, Grady has learned. They show less interest when it's just him and not him and Nico, but a scattered few hang around this bright weekday morning when Grady's Southern politeness reflex takes over: He smiles and waves and wishes them a pleasant day. He has a meeting with Vince, his publicist, and his media coordinator to plan interviews and potential tour stops and promo ideas. And now, how to best handle the media storm over his engagement. Later on, he's meeting with Duke to discuss the changes he's making to the single and what to release instead while Grady continues to put off actually making any changes to the single. Vince is supposed to go along to Stomp Records with him, but he looks so harassed after they discuss how to put out the fires from the wedding leak that Grady gives him the rest of the day off. The meeting with Duke is just a quick check-in anyhow.

Grady picks up an afternoon snack at the custard place he loves; there's a long line and it's crowded, though everyone seems to be more concerned with their custard than with him. A small mercy, but he'll take it. While he waits, he sends Clementine a video of cats with balloons stuck to their fur. *Come see me,* she texts back, along with an address.

"I'll take a pralines and cream, please. Oh, Valencia! Haven't seen you here in a while."

"Grady! Well, you hardly come in these days!" Valencia has been managing the custard place for as long as Grady's been stopping in. She's not always in the front, but, when she is, she'll chat with Grady as if he's just any other regular customer.

Grady slumps over the counter on his elbow and says dramatically, "Tell me about it. My fiancé has me on a worse diet than my trainer ever did." She beams at him, then turns to get his custard ready. It trips on his tongue a bit, *fiancé,* but it is such a relief to talk about it. That everyone knows doesn't seem like a complete disaster to him. It's always been harder for Nico, not just sharing their lives, but the lack of control over what gets shared when. Valencia brings the cup back and puts a lid on it, then rings him up.

"How's the little one?" Grady asks as he pulls out his wallet.

"Starting Pre-K in the fall." She takes the cash, and Grady puts his change in the tip jar. "Can you believe that?"

"I certainly cannot, not when I swear you were just showing me the pictures of her first steps!" As he's putting his wallet back, Grady's phone beeps with another text.

Clem: If you're getting food bring me some.

He orders a butterscotch custard to go, and adds more money to the tip jar to make up for all the trouble he's causing. "Thanks, Valencia, have a good one. You tell that girl to stop growin' up so fast!"

"I will! Don't be a stranger, okay? And congrats!"

The address he goes to is in the same downtown area, so the custard is only a little soupy by the time he finds it. The small brick building turns out to be another recording studio, this one even more cramped, with Clem at the controls again and a musician he doesn't recognize in the booth. Grady sets the custard and plastic spoon down in front of her. "Again? Who'd you sweet-talk for studio space for your new protégé this time?"

She waves him off with the spoon and pulls the lid free. "An associate."

She is so unnecessarily mysterious sometimes. "And this is…"

"This is Joaquin." She flips a switch so Grady can hear the music they just recorded. The kid in the booth is wearing a cowboy hat over his headphones and the kind of fancy shirt Nico would own: high-quality detailing and an unusual bright print with a bowtie to top it off. He has a low-country honky-tonk sound that Grady digs right away, and he's young and cute to boot. "He's great. No one will sign him?" That voice has a ton of potential for a broad range of listeners.

Clem pushes a button. "Joaquin, sugar. Why won't anyone sign you?"

He talks into the screen covering the mic. "Too weird, too brown, too gay. Take your pick." Then he gasps and yanks off both the headphones and his hat and rushes from the booth. "What? *Grady Dawson*, no, you are not here right now!"

Clem winks and leans back in her chair to eat her custard. "He wanted to meet you."

Grady holds out his hand. "Well, it's entirely my pleasure, Joaquin. You were really incredible in there—" Joaquin grasps his hand and shakes it while bouncing up and down.

"You are *such* an inspiration for me! I'm dying right now, literally dead. You and Nico are amazing, like bae goals, seriously." He looks over to Clem with his eyes popped wide and makes a high-pitched squealing noise.

Grady chuckles. "Oh. Thanks, I guess."

Grady stays to listen for another song, and Clem explains his story. Like Ellis, he's having some trouble booking gigs and getting signed. He came all the way from Florida to chase his dreams in Nashville, and Clem wants to give him a fighting chance.

"I'm guessing you didn't find him at a lady bar."

"Busking," Clem says, then mashes a button. "Five minutes, doll, and then they're chasing us out of here." Grady has to take off before then if he wants to make his meeting, so he waves to Joaquin, then sends him a grin and a wink just to see if he'll squeal in delight. He does. Then he leans down to quickly kiss Clem on the cheek. "You keep all this up and you'll need your own studio and record company soon," he teases as he leaves.

Grady hustles to Stomp's headquarters, runs up the stairs when the elevator takes too long, and arrives out of breath and with one single minute to spare. There's a new receptionist again, a younger one, who hands Grady a heavy manila envelope instead of buzzing Duke to let him know Grady has arrived. "Ah, I'm sorry. I thought I had a meeting."

She lifts one hand and wiggles her fingers at the envelope. "He's not here, and that is, so." Then she turns away, inviting no further conversation.

He reads the contents of the envelope in the car, which is a mistake. He's not quite sure how he gets home in one piece, but he does, coasting past the now-large crowd gathered near the driveway, who yell and take pictures, then into the garage, where he sits in his truck. It's more humid in there than outside. Sweat prickles at his temples and the back of his neck; his shirt clings to his back. He drove home on automatic with a million thoughts racing. He just wanted to get home so he could sort everything out. Now that he's home, his brain is stuffed with static, and he can't think through anything at all. He spots the box on a shelf with old paint cans and bug spray, grabs it, and strides to the back deck. The fate of the box and its contents is suddenly his most urgent concern.

In the pit out back, he builds a fire and sheds his shirt when the wood catches; it's so hot, he's like a pig roasting on a spit. Then he sits on the bench and flips open the shoebox lid. The stuff inside is random and worthless: a punch card for a sandwich shop, some fishing hooks, a birthday card signed by someone named Tori, a ticket stub from a Vols football game, a Zippo lighter, a vintage car magazine. He finds nothing of worth, nothing that would tell him more about his father than the little he already knew. Why Clay kept all this, he doesn't know. Why Grady put it aside so he could pretend it might be something worth keeping, he really doesn't know. Grady pulls out the magazine to toss it in the fire. It's folded in half and dog-eared in several places. Grady flips through it. And then, a sudden flash of a memory surprises him—something he missed that was hidden under the magazine.

"So, this is new." Nico says from the open back door. Grady didn't hear him come home. "Kind of hot for a fire, isn't it?"

"I was gonna burn all this stuff." Grady opens the top of the slim brown carton in his hand, and Nico sits next to him on the bench. "I remember him smoking these. The smell." He holds the Swisher Sweet cigarillos to his nose and inhales, then fishes the lighter out of the shoebox. After he lights one and pulls on it a few times, he offers the box to Nico, who hesitates, purses his lips, then slowly pulls out a cigarillo.

"Light?" Grady holds out the Zippo lighter; the silver metal catches the bright sun. Nico shakes his head and inspects the cigarillo as if it contains secrets or an explanation for Grady's behavior. "I remember... I was in the back of a car," Grady explains. "It was big. I think, the car, but then I wasn't, so it's hard to say. They were both in the front, my parents, and he was smoking one of these. Vaughn. My dad." Grady takes another drag of the Swisher Sweet, but he's unused to the acrid burn of smoke in his throat and lungs these days, and it makes him cough until his eyes water. He pulls the cigarillo away from his lips and watches the ember grow and the sweet smoke curl into the darker smoke of the fire. "He was there. I remember him."

"You were really planning on burning all of it?"

It's so much when Nico looks at him like that, those dark, dark eyes that make him feel bared and seen and as though he should fall to his knees at Nico's feet. Grady nods and he knows it's time to stop hiding, from himself, from his pain. "I thought I had more time." Grady watches the ember burn the cigarillo smaller and smaller. "I threw money at him but I— It was just easier than dealing with him, and now it's too late, and I'm a bad person, too, you know? I didn't care. I didn't care if he died, Nico." Nico tosses both Swisher Sweets into the fire pit, Grady's lit and his still not lit, but it burns plenty now. He pulls Grady against him and strokes through Grady's hair.

"Oh, Grady."

They're both sweating; it is much too hot for a fire. Grady can't do it anyway, can't burn it all as if that will change anything, as if it can undo anything. It's all that's left of Vaughn Dawson now, and turning it to ash won't change his or Grady's mistakes. Grady pulls away from Nico's embrace, puts the contents back in the shoebox, closes the lid, takes a breath, and says, "Nico, I'm in trouble."

Grady Dawson vs. Stomp Records

Country Scoop Daily

By Austin Boyd

Stomp Records has filed a breach-of-contract suit against country singer Grady Dawson, claiming he has refused to deliver a third album as requested, and that Dawson violated the exclusivity clause of this contract by performing an unreleased song in a public venue without prior permission. (See fan-captured video of the performance here.) In addition to demanding a finished album, Stomp is seeking to bar Dawson from public performances until he complies.

In a statement released by Vince Bauer, Dawson's manager, the singer says that he has in fact submitted an album titled Blended Notes, *but that the label refuses to release the album due to "creative differences." Bauer told* Country Scoop Daily *that Grady Dawson has, "fulfilled the terms of his contract and then some. This is about control and nothing more."*

Grady Dawson Files Countersuit against Stomp Records
Music News Now
By Kendra Jones

Grady Dawson has filed a countersuit against Stomp Records in response to a breach of contract filing by the record company, saying that Stomp is forcing Dawson to remain in career limbo. He is seeking to be released from the label, to have the exclusive rights to his songs returned to him, and to be legally free to sign with another record label.

"After an incredibly successful recording career that has provided unprecedented success for both parties, Stomp Records has taken actions that are stalling and irreparably damaging Grady Dawson's career," a spokesman for Dawson said. "It is with great regret that he has been forced to file a countersuit, but the label has left him with no other option."

Grady Dawson: Wedding Off Amid Legal Troubles?
StarzBuzz Magazine
By Cat Palaver

Grady Dawson and stylist fiancé Nico Takahashi may have cancelled their wedding due to Grady's on-going legal battles with his record label. According to rumors, the maybe-not-engaged couple cancelled their wedding cake and have not been seen making wedding plans for some time. According to our source, "They're never seen leaving the house together. I'm not sure if Grady is even living there now."

This isn't the first time Grady has been in hot water professionally or personally. For everyone who claimed Grady Dawson was a wild stallion who would never really settle down: Looks like you were right all along.

"Wild stallion. Really?" Nico steals a bite of Thit Bo Luc Lac from the takeout container on Grady's lap, tipping his computer over into the space between them on the bed.

Grady sets it upright, scowling at the bright colors and shouting headlines on the website. "Why you read these gossip sites..."

"Know your enemy." Nico taps his chopsticks against his temple, and a little bit of beef and watercress from Grady's dinner falls onto the duvet. "And they aren't *entirely* wrong about everything," Nico points out, scooping up the blob of dropped food.

No, they aren't entirely wrong. As a matter of fact, the first two articles Nico read out loud as they ate takeout in bed after Nico got home from work—and Grady spent another restless day at home like a princess locked in a tower—were spot on. But, "The wedding hasn't been cancelled. Just... reconsidered."

Nico chews his shrimp and rice noodles. "Right. And if the label shakes us down for thirty mil like they're trying to, we'll be *reconsidering* right down to the Justice of Peace." He says it lightly, pops food into his mouth, and leans back on a pile of pillows. He can say it as casually as he wants to, Grady knows without a doubt that this whole thing is killing Nico. The lawsuits and the media circus has only gotten more frantic with each passing day, and now the threat of bankruptcy and the end of Grady's career looms over them. No matter how many times Nico reassures him that it's not true, Grady is still convinced that he's failed him in every way. No matter how many times he apologizes for not telling Nico right away, he just can't accept Nico's forgiveness.

And, at the advice of his new, extremely expensive lawyer, Grady has been lying low: not appearing in public, lest he be asked to make a statement that could further complicate things or be seen as making a public appearance he hasn't been approved to make, as if he can't be trusted to leave the house. When he was young and naive and just thrilled to be signed to a label, Grady certainly hadn't realized he was granting Stomp Records ownership of *him*. And at the time, either no one he was associated with knew any better, or they just didn't care enough to tell him. His new, very accomplished lawyer has warned him that litigation could drag on for months, if not years, and, in the meantime, Grady is convinced he will slowly descend into madness.

Grady sets his Vietnamese takeout on his nightstand and drops dramatically backward across the bed so his head lands on Nico's stretched-out legs. "I messed everything up."

"You didn't do anything." Nico uses Grady's bare chest as a table for his take out container. "Duke and the label are trying to fuck you over. Well, fuck them." He stabs a chopstick into the container, and it pokes Grady's ribs through the thin waxed cardboard.

"I shoulda just fixed the song like they wanted in the first place." Careful not to upset the food carton, he shifts to look up at Nico. "I've been in this business long enough to know how it works. It's just askin' for trouble to refuse them."

"Nothing matters to you more than your integrity as an artist." Nico moves the food and sets the laptop on Grady's chest. It's even warmer than the food and hums vibrations against his skin. "It's worth fighting for."

Integrity. It's what he's clung to when he had nothing else worth holding, when he felt worthless himself. Does it really matter as much as it used to, when he has so much? Did he have integrity in the first place, or was that just a lie he told himself to feel worthy of *something*. "Is my integrity worth thirty million dollars?"

Nico presses his mouth flat. Grady watches him scroll and click and pull faces at whatever he's reading. Then his eyebrows shoot up, and his head cocks sharply. "Oh, here we go: 'Fan outcry amid label dispute. ' Grady cranes his head to see.

Grady Dawson Fans Bombard Stomp Records
EntertainNET
By Jo Ames

It helps to have die-hard fans in a cutthroat business and, for Grady Dawson, it helps even more if those fans are loud and relentless on social media. After learning that Dawson's upcoming album **Blended Notes** *is being held in purgatory following "creative differences" with Stomp Records and that Dawson has filed a countersuit stating the label is "irreparably damaging his career," fans are joining the fight in order to get the much-anticipated album released. "We've waited a long time for this album," says a fan I spoke to on Twitter. "But more than that we support Grady and believe in his vision for his own music."*

In a matter of days, there was a trending hashtag: #ReleaseGradyNow, an online petition already more than 200,000 signatures strong, a website, and a call to boycott Stompfest, the Stomp Records annual end-of-summer festival in downtown Nashville that draws hundreds of thousands of fans each year. Grady Dawson had to withdraw his scheduled appearance at Stompfest, as he is currently barred from public performances.

"Grady has always made us feel loved and important," another fan told me. "And it's time for us to make sure we return the favor."

Buy a #ReleaseGradyNow T-shirt here, and 100% of the profits will be donated to the campaign's efforts.

"Did you know about this?" Nico asks, as Grady reads the article a third time, still trying to believe it's actually all true.

"No," he says. "Why would they do all this?"

Nico *tsks* and closes the laptop. "Because they love you. I can't even hope to love you as much as they do."

"That's not—"

Nico shakes his head. "It's fine, I've made my peace with it." He takes the laptop off of Grady's chest, flips back the duvet, and slides down on the mattress next to him with his hand spreading low on Grady's bared stomach. "I have ways of comforting myself."

Grady hums and moves in. The intimacy they share has always been intense, always shattering in the best way. Now it's the only thing in his life that is safe and steady. Nico and the way he loves him—it's all he has that isn't rapidly turning to dust. Grady traces the lines of his love onto Nico's skin. It's the only thing he has left to offer.

19

Grady's daily routine keeps him sane for a while: Wake up early, jog back and forth on the little path in the woods behind their house, make Nico breakfast, work out in their weight room, take a long shower, tinker in the music room, tinker with the Superbird, call Amy, go for another run in the woods, take another shower, decide on takeout for dinner, wait for Nico. This morning, though, as Grady wakes to the bedroom softly glowing with the first light of morning, he just can't find the energy to get out of bed and retrieve his jogging shorts. He lies there watching the room get brighter and brighter, staring at the wall, at the ceiling, at Nico sleeping burrowed under the covers.

Nico's alarm goes off, and he silences it. It goes off again a few minutes later, and he blindly slaps at it until it goes silent. He does that three more times before finally grumbling off to the shower with his eyes closed and face screwed tight with indignation. It's cute; Grady's sad that he usually misses this part of Nico's morning and also worries about how often he must run into walls with his eyes shut tight like that. Grady rolls over and listens to the shower run, the buzz of Nico's electric razor, the water running in the sink as he brushes his teeth.

"Are you feeling okay?" Nico pauses, coming out of the walk-in closet with clothes draped over his arm.

Is he? Maybe that's why he can't get out bed, though he doesn't seem to have any other symptoms. "I dunno. Might be comin' down with something?"

Nico pulls on slacks and walks over to the bed to place his palm on Grady's forehead. "No fever, that's good." His forehead is creased with worry lines as he shrugs into his shirt. "Want me to pick something up from the drugstore?"

It's unlikely the drugstore sells anything that would help Grady with his current ills. "Nah, I'm okay."

"Okay." Nico kisses his forehead. "Just let me know if you change your mind. I'm heading in now; hit the snooze button too many times." He stands, loops his tie around the back of his neck and glances down Grady's body under the covers. "Unless you want to have a quickie? I'm already running late, so what's ten more minutes?"

Grady shifts, curls his legs up and rubs his face into the pillow. "Nah, go on ahead."

The worry lines reappear. "Okay. I'll see you later."

The garage door rumbles open and closed, and Grady sits up in alarm. He just turned down a morning quickie. He rubs at his eyes, trying to shake the heavy melancholy from his head, then forces his body out of bed. What *is* wrong with him?

It takes him longer than usual, but he does pull on his jogging shorts, then his sneakers. He picks up his phone and earbuds and heads to the kitchen to get water, but as he's filling the bottle, it all becomes too much bother. It's too hot now, and the path will be too busy; he can't decide on music to run to, and he overdid it on squats and lunges yesterday anyhow. He could play around on his guitar, maybe try some new songs to wake up his muse, but, if Duke and Stomp Records have their way, he may never play professionally again. The thought is so depressing, he can't bear to touch his guitar. And he can't spend one more frustrating day on that damn car that refuses to show any sign of life. Even knitting is too much to deal with.

He was wrong, Grady realizes, as he flops on the couch to flip through their seldom-used TV in the living room. He's not slowly going insane; he's quickly losing the will to live. He may not be a wild stallion, but he sure as hell feels like a trapped animal, one that's given up the fight to ever be free again.

"Isn't this where I left you?"

Nico finds him in bed. Grady was more bored than tired, but bed seemed to be the only place he could stand being, even with the sun still hanging on, low and soft in the sky. Nico checks his forehead, makes a perplexed sort of *hmm*, and disappears. When he comes back, he sets a mug and saucer on Grady's side table.

"Fresh ginger tea. Whatever's going on with you, that should help."

"I'll let it cool," Grady says, watching the steam curl from the cup while Nico unwinds and undresses in the bathroom, then sits, quietly busy on his tablet, on the chaise longue in their bedroom as the sky darkens. When he comes to bed, he settles close behind Grady with his naked torso pressed to Grady's back. He drags his lips across Grady's shoulder and neck and jaw. Grady can't look away from the tea that's gone cold, can't make himself respond, even though he wants to. He *wants* to want to. Nico sighs and leaves one last lingering kiss on Grady's temple before flipping to his side away from Grady. "Good night."

"Night."

Just before he falls asleep, Grady has a panicked moment of realization that he could very well lose Nico, too. His strangely sluggish mind just now comes to grips with the possibility. Even worse is the realization that maybe that would be best. Every time his world has gone to hell, Grady has been alone with no one to drag down with him. Is that that the way it has to be? His mind starts to tie itself in knots again, and, despite being exhausted all day, Grady tosses and turns for hours.

The next day Grady does manage to get to the deck, ready for his run. He sits to tighten his laces, and then gets lost watching the leaves sway in musical patterns. He lies back on the wooden bench to watch them. Just for a bit. Just a little longer now.

"There you are. Jesus, shit, this house has entirely too many stairs." It's Gwen. He doesn't turn away from the dancing leaves or sit up.

"Nico send you to check on me?"

Her heavy combat boot footsteps approach the bench; her shadow falls across his body. "I'll have you know I came here to harass you of my accord." Gwen moves until she's blocking his view of the trees. Grady squints up at her. She sets her hands on her sharp little hips and gives him a worried look an awful lot like the one Nico keeps directing at him. "So things suck, huh?"

"Yup."

"Well, they've sucked before. And they'll suck again." She drops her hands to her sides and rocks up and down on her toes. "That's life. It sucks."

Grady flings his arm over his eyes. The sun is too bright; looking at Gwen is too much effort. "This is a terrible pep talk." There's a dull thump on the foot that he has draped over the side of the bench. "Why are you kicking me?"

"I kick you when you need to be kicked. Now, come on. I'm missing time with my kid for this. Up." At that, Grady does sit up. And he is happy to see her, even with her kicking him and her pissed off expression and all, as if some life has been returned to him just because of her company. "Okay, I'm up."

"Super," Gwen replies sarcastically. "Now go put a damn shirt on. And different shorts. My god, man, those are *obscene*. Do you go out in public with those? Did Nico buy them for you? I bet he did, horndog—" She continues harassing him into the house, until he jogs upstairs to shower and change, smiling a little as he goes.

When he comes down, she hands him a ukulele and a guitar zipped into their soft cases, and then a hat and sunglasses. "We're leaving?" Grady puts on the dark glasses and ball cap and hauls the instruments over both shoulders.

"Oh, yeah. I know I'd be climbing the walls by now if I were you, so I'm busting you out for the afternoon." She twirls car keys on her finger and walks backward to the door.

"What about the paparazzi?"

"Don't even worry about it." She makes the sort of face that will immediately set Nico on edge but Grady loves. Gwen may have settled down some, matured into life with a wife and a kid, but you can never entirely take the rebel out the girl. Grady grins, and follows her. At the end of the driveway, Gwen rolls down both the driver's and Grady's passenger side window and says, "Take the wheel."

Grady sinks down, pulling the bill of the hat low over his face. "What?"

"Take. The wheel." She lets go of the steering wheel entirely, leaving Grady no choice but to steer the car lest they crash into the tall pine trees lining the edge of their property.

"What are you doing?" Grady asks, though he can see for himself: She has both arms outstretched, leaning all the way out of her window, then leaning over to the passenger side, crushing Grady against the seat and almost completely blocking his view of the road as she flips off the paparazzi and their flashing cameras when they come thundering out onto the road.

She bounces back into her seat, takes control of the steering wheel, and cackles. "I read somewhere they can't print the pictures with that. I've wanted to try it for a while now, honestly."

They've made it out of sight of the cameras, so Grady sits up, laughing and shaking his head. "That's true for print, but anything goes on the Internet, you know."

Gwen pouts. "Oh. Bummer. Well, it was still fun." She turns to him, a little guilty. "Will you get in trouble?"

He's staying home under advisement and good sense and maybe a little bit because of his own unwillingness to deal with his life right now, but he is not actually a prisoner in his own home. Still, his career may be over, his reputation is once again sunk in the mud, his marriage may be put off indefinitely, and his family of origin remains in shambles, only more so. "How much more trouble could I possibly get into?"

Gwen smirks. "That sounds like a challenge."

Gwen drives them to a quiet family suburb where she parks in a complex with a green park, busy outdoor pool, large public library, and community center; all of them look new and upscale. The air is cooled slightly by a breeze—though it's still plenty hot outside—and the soft rustling of the wind is punctuated by the sounds of kids laughing and playing.

"What's happening here?" Grady asks, as Gwen leads him to the community center on the back side of the municipal complex.

"This is where we take Cayo for music classes," Gwen says, opening the door to a wide air-conditioned hallway where the same happy sounds of children fill the space. "Or where I pay one hundred fifty bucks a month for Cayo to watch some hippie lady sing 'The Itsy Bitsy Spider' and shake a maraca." She stops in front of a door painted with a colorful sign that reads: *Play On.* "Anyway, they also do music therapy and low-cost lessons for special needs and low income kids. And I thought it seemed like your kind of deal." She nods at the instruments on Grady's shoulders.

Grady hesitates when she goes to open the door; getting out of the house and spending time with Gwen is one thing, but he doesn't know if he's quite up to entertaining a group of kids. What if he ends up just sitting there staring off into space as he's been doing so much lately? What if he's not allowed to do this? Gwen must sense his hesitation, because she moves away from the door and motions for Grady to do the same.

"Listen. I know our situations are different. Your parents were no-shows your whole life, and mine are just kind of generally awful." She shrugs as she says it, as if she doesn't really care, but she looks at her boots and bites hard on her bottom lip before continuing. "I get it, though. Being conflicted. I've thought about how I would feel if my mom kicked it—" She cringes. "Sorry, passed away. I just— Whatever you're feeling, or not feeling, it's okay. Shit's complicated, right?" Gwen looks up, and it's hard to deny those big blue eyes of hers, the impish nose and mouth, though it's so much more complex than his absentee father passing away. "And remember, you're not alone," she says, "so don't jump off of any buildings or try to join a convent again."

Grady chuckles. "I was never gonna join a convent in the first place, Short Stuff."

"So you say." She reaches up to punch his arm. "Just promise me that if you do decide to do anything crazy, you'll call me first, so I can do it with you."

"Deal," Grady says and slings his arm over her little shoulders as they walk into the music center. Grady has barely taken in the bright walls decorated with music notes, the rainbow-striped carpet, and instruments on shelves and in baskets, before he's rushed by two little boys who attach themselves to his legs.

"Can I play your guitar?" The one in the dinosaur T-shirt grabs for the case.

The one with a bandage on his chin says, "No, I wanna play first; can I play first?"

Gwen offers no help, just laughs, and Grady can't exactly move with two kids hanging on his legs like barnacles. "Now hold on a minute," he says with a smile. They're sweet—grabby, but sweet. Soon most of the kids in the center are gathering close, curious and excited about having a visitor. He's played for kids before, but Grady is used to playing in children's hospitals and wards, which are subdued by necessity.

An exaggerated sing-song voice announces, "*Okay*, my friends. Everyone *sit* on a color so we can get *started*, please!" The kids scatter, and a woman with her hair twisted up in a purple scarf approaches Grady. "Hello, I'm Bethany." She shakes his hand, and the silver bracelets covering half of her forearms jingle melodically.

"Grady." And if there's a flash of recognition, she covers it quickly, welcoming him to the center as "Cayo's Mommy's friend." Behind her shoulder, Gwen mouths, "hippie lady," and points to Bethany.

"Thank you so much for having me. This is really great, what you're doing here." Grady tips his head toward her and grins, and Bethany blushes before showing him to a short chair in front of the rainbow carpet.

"My *friends*, we have *new* friend today! Can *everyone* say 'hi, Grady!'"

"Hi, Grady!" The group shouts.

Bethany continues in the same emphatic sing-song voice, "Grady is going to sing us some songs, so everyone may stand and pick *one* instrument and *one* ribbon. If all my friends sitting on *orange* can *walk* to the baskets, please."

Row by colorful row the kids come up to claim a ribbon on a stick and a percussion instrument, choosing from tambourines, rhythm sticks, hand drums, bells, castanets, xylophones, and maracas. Grady marvels at Bethany's continued patience and enthusiasm. Not a one of these kids can be over the age of five, and they're all incredibly eager and excited, and, with every new instrument snatched from the basket, *loud*. Bethany gets them to quiet down, then she and Gwen join the kids on a yellow and a purple stripe, respectively, and Grady—

Grady has a moment of stage fright. He's played stadiums; he's played for politicians and celebrities and on live television, yet none of those were as intimidating as two dozen preschoolers with their eyes agog and tambourines at the ready. Kids are brutally honest. If they hate it they'll say so; if they're bored they'll leave. They have no biases, no expectations, and no cynicism. Grady unzips his ukulele and sets it timidly on his chest.

"So. I um. I like playin' the ukulele," he starts, plinking a few strings to tune them. "Because to me, it sounds happy." The kids stare at him. One little girl hits her maraca on the carpet like a hammer until Bethany stops her. "Um," Grady says.

A little boy with red hair says, "Violins sound sad."

Grady considers this. "They do sound sad, don't they?" A little girl with braids and plastic barrettes in her hair raises her hand.

"The one like this—" She places both hands to the side of her head and wiggles her fingers. "*Toot-toot-toot*. That's happy, too."

"A flute?" Grady guesses, and she wiggles happily. "That sounds… joyful. You're right." Then every single kid wants to share what instruments sound happy. They loudly offer bells, xylophone, tambourine, piano, banjo, cymbals as examples. One kid shouts "farts," and, after the uproarious laughter dies down, Grady suggests tuba as an alternative. The sad instruments are named: piano too, sometimes, guitar, saxophone, harp, and, at the red-haired boy's insistence, maracas, because they "sound like snakes."

"How about we sing a song about being happy, then," Grady says and launches into "Happy and You Know It." All of his anxiousness is now gone and his doldrums, too. The best part of a kid's honestly is that it's pure. They want nothing from Grady but music and to enjoy themselves. They don't have expectations about who he is or should be, they don't care one whit about his personal life or his legal troubles, they aren't gonna take a video of him and broadcast it as far and wide as they can for bragging rights. These kids just sing and bang away on their hand drums and wave their ribbons. And just as after a quiet session with kids stuck in hospital beds fighting for their lives, when Grady leaves, his problems seem so much smaller, and the world seems filled with joy and hope.

"Thank you," Grady tells Gwen on their way back.

Gwen wriggles her shoulders. "I'm awesome; you can say it."

Grady looks over seriously. "You're awesome. And I really needed that."

"Aw, Grady." She pats his hand. "Be gentle with yourself, okay."

He watches the leaves zoom by as Gwen drives him back to the house for another bout of detainment. "I'm tryin'."

21

Nico has been working long hours and longer weeks, and tonight is no different. He has an event that keeps him out long past when Grady gives up and goes to sleep, then he's gone by the time Grady wakes up. The only lingering reminders of him are wrinkled sheets on Nico's side of their bed and the heap of designer clothes on top of the hamper. Grady slips the clothes into the hamper. He stops to pass his thumb over the fabric of a black summer-weight button-down. Nico looks good in it; the sleeves sit snugly on his biceps, and it highlights the agile lines of his shoulders. Grady drops the shirt into the hamper. This morning he's able to shake off the gloom long enough to manage a run. His feet pad on the dirt path, as the heat grows thicker and more oppressive; he's drenched with sweat by the time he's finally satisfied with the distance he's run and the ache in his muscles.

He starts off lighter today, happier, but the gray moves back in like a dark cloud as he faces another lonely, restless, unproductive day in the house. Grady is on the couch air drying from his shower and aimlessly switching TV channels when the doorbell rings. For a second, as he's grabbing clothes from upstairs and dashing back down, he's sure that one of the paparazzi from the permanent camp outside has gotten ballsy enough to come right to the door. And then, as he's cracking the door open, he worries that he's being served with yet another lawsuit.

"Clay. Hey, good morning."

"Mornin'." Clay scratches his ear and glances around the front porch; in his other hand is a tool box. "I was repairing some roof shingles nearby. Thought I'd stop in."

Grady had asked him to come by and fix some stuff around the house; that's right. "Oh, sure," Grady says, as though he hadn't completely forgotten. "Come right in. Slip your shoes off, if you don't terribly mind." Clay does, then limps in slowly but with determination, and Grady mentally scans the house for something Clay could work on. *Move-in-ready* was very high on Nico's list when they were house hunting. "You know, the ice maker is finicky," Grady says, pointing the way to the kitchen. "It either makes way too much or barely anything at all. I dunno if it's a sensor, or it just can't pace itself."

Clay doesn't acknowledge Grady's joke. "Is the motor running when it's not making any ice?" He sets his toolbox down on the counter next to the fridge.

"I'm not sure," Grady says, opening the freezer. Inside there's ice cream and frozen fruit and ice cubes scattered across the bottom.

"Could be the water valve. Or the central circuit's gone bad."

And here Grady thought the ice maker maybe had a tendency to get overexcited. He leans back on the counter while Clay tinkers inside the freezer. Grady doesn't know much about him, Uncle Clay. He's Vaughn's father's brother. He's a handyman. Never married, as far as Grady knows. That whole Dawson family is a mystery to him, despite his last name. He's been stubborn about getting to know them; after all, they didn't make any effort to know him. This part of his history is a blank space.

"You always worked for yourself?"

"No. For a building company for a while. Contractor. Till I was too old and slow to keep up." He adjusts something with pliers. "Been workin' for myself for a while now."

It can't be easy trying to keep his head above water working as a handyman with two knees barely keeping him upright. Grady can't believe he was up on a roof today; that took some serious stubborn determination. "Vaughn ever help you out?"

The ice maker whirrs, and Clay shuts the freezer door. "All set." He drops the tools back into the bulky metal box. "Vaughn did his own thing. Never could pin down what that boy was up to." *Nothing good*, Grady thinks, but he leaves it unsaid. Clay's memories of Vaughn are his own; Grady doesn't want to soil them. He's glad his father had someone who cared if he had a roof over his head from time to time. There's a wobbly handrail on the top step upstairs, but Grady doesn't want Clay climbing those stairs with his bad knees. If they go around outside, it shouldn't be too difficult for him to get to the garage. "Say, you know anything about cars?"

Clay says he knows a little, enough to keep things running, and the look of consternation on his face when Grady shows him the Superbird indicates that the old hunk of rust may be worse off than Grady thought. "Hopeless?" Grady frowns at the busted engine.

Clay just says, "Well."

The car isn't even good for the parts that have been left in; everything is rusted or corroded. The poor old broad was left out to fend for herself and rot away all alone. But Grady just can't give up on her. He morosely pulls at a loose bolt and screw.

"Body's solid," Clay says. "She ain't pretty but—could still work." Clay closes the hood as if he's embarrassed on the car's behalf, having exposed all its problems to the world like that.

"You think?"

"Oh, sure. May have to gut the rest of it and start all over. But the frame is good."

Grady offers Clay a drink, and they walk back to the kitchen at Clay's shuffling pace. They pass the music room and home gym. "You sing, right? Vaughn mentioned that."

"That's right." Grady pauses, knocked unsteady; his father talked about him, his father talked about what he does.

"His mama was a singer for a time, Vaughn. Her and her sisters. Had a stage act and all."

"Really?" He'd had no idea. Memaw could sing and play some instruments. Grady always figured his musical tendencies came from her. Back in the kitchen, Grady gets two glasses and ice from the now-functional ice maker and pours them both some sweet tea. "What was her name?"

Clay takes the glass from Grady and nods his thanks. "Lyle. Emmeline Lyle."

Grady sees Clay off to his car, after learning Emmeline's sisters' names and that Clay has scheduled his knee replacement surgery. "I'm glad to hear it," Grady tells him, hunched next to door of Clay's bulky sedan. "Remember to send me the bill." Clay will be out of work for some time following the surgery, and not working means no money, because he works for himself. Grady can't let that happen, though it's not likely Clay will take money from him. "I'm having Vaughn's car fixed up," Grady ventures. "Why don't I send it back to you so you can sell it?"

"Oh, that's all right," Clay says, busying himself with adjusting the air-conditioning vents and rearview mirror. "It's rightfully yours."

Grady shades his eyes from the sun and leans farther down. "If I bring one more junk car into the garage, Nico's gonna have my head. You'd be doin' me a favor."

Clay considers it, then nods his slow nod. "All right."

"All right." Grady stands, taps the hood of the car, and sends him on his way. He can't imagine what Clay thinks about the gang of cameramen parked at the end of the driveway. He probably doesn't care to think much about it all—someone like Clay, who is sensible and practical and down-to-earth certainly has no use for gossip magazines. He reminds Grady of his granddaddy in that way, though Granddaddy had a rascally streak that kept Memaw on her toes.

That evening, he takes takeout leftovers up to their home office and searches the Internet for Emmeline Lyle and her sisters Glory, Josephine, and Maribelle. After hours of digging, he finds only that The Lyle Sisters once worked with legendary bluegrass singers The Blue Mood back in the late '60s. Filling in the pieces like this, finding something of himself in a person he never got the chance to meet, should be exciting. Mostly, though, he's bitter. Vaughn didn't just deprive Grady of a father, but of a whole family, a whole history. If Grady had known about his grandmother, would that have changed things? Would he have tried harder to have a relationship with Vaughn? Could they have found a common ground? Could music have saved Vaughn as it did Grady? Grady closes the laptop and gathers his dishes. It's too late; it's always too late for him.

22

Grady starts a new day with a song stuck in his head, as if he dreamed it to life—the same two lines of notes in a loop—and it's only after he rises with the sun to jog in the woods, lifts weights and showers and then stops to fix the loose railing upstairs himself, that it dawns on him. It isn't a song he knows; it's not one he's written or performed before. He pauses on the bottom step, twists the screwdriver, runs the notes over again— Yep, that's new. And if a song refuses to leave him alone, he's gonna write it down and compose something sooner or later. Once the railing is tightened, he has nothing else on his agenda, so it may as well be sooner.

Grady drops the screwdriver onto the coffee table in the living room, searches for a paper and pen, and finds neither. Thinking, he puffs his cheeks out, then blows out a frustrated breath and heads upstairs. The song rolls over and over, more insistently now that he's paying attention to it, more urgently with every passing beat.

"Oh, what are you doing here?"

Nico doesn't turn from the desk, but he does startle and slam the laptop closed. "I don't know how many times I have to explain to you that I live here," he remarks, his shoulders held stiff and high: a tell.

"No, I meant—" Grady moves close enough behind him to see the snarky quirk of one eyebrow. "I meant why aren't you at work?"

Nico pivots to the side with his legs sharply crossed. "Gwen was…" He tilts his head in annoyance, "…concerned that I was spending too much time at work and avoiding you." He blinks as if to gather patience. "Though she phrased it in a less diplomatic way."

A grin tugs Grady's lips; he's sure she did. Down the hall in their bedroom, Grady's phone rings. "Oh, shoot, I was supposed to call your mom right about now." He'd been sidetracked by that song. That *song*. Grady grabs a notepad and pen, drops sideways onto the weird orange chair, draws a rough staff and clef, then starts to fill in the notes he keeps hearing. Nico's phone goes off.

"Yes, I'm with him," Nico says after taking the call, instead of "hello." Grady can tell Nico's eyes are on him as he scribbles down the bones of a song. "I'm honestly not sure," Nico says to the phone, then, "I *am*… Okay… I will ask him… I like how you never call me anymore by the way… Sure, sure…" Grady looks up when Nico goes quiet and his face shifts through several expressions as he listens to whatever Amy is saying. "Okay. Love you, too." He sets his phone down and stretches, then says to Grady, "Daily phone calls, huh?"

Grady erases a G-flat and replaces it with an F-sharp. "We have nice chats."

"About?" The eyebrow rises anew.

Grady loops the song in his head and adds a few more notes. "Your brother. Gardening. You. Your dad. Doctor Oz." Grady taps a beat in 3/4 time with the end of his pen; his eyes dance over the notes. "Did you know thousands of Americans have fatty livers?"

"What does that even—" Nico walks over to him. "You know what I don't actually want to know. What are you working on?"

Grady marks down some chords, after moving his fingers in place as if pressing the corresponding strings on his guitar. "I think it's a lullaby," he says.

Nico scans the notes, then Grady's eyes. "Will you play it for me?"

The first time he played a song for Nico in his old house, in the basement he used as a practice space then, he felt as if Nico saw him, really saw *him*, and all Grady wanted to do was keep showing him, offering piece after piece of his fragmented heart, as if he knew then somehow that Nico would be the one to help him put it back together. "Soon," Grady answers. "It's not ready yet."

Nico skims over his hair, fleeting and soft. "Okay. Oh, she wanted to know whose tuxedo she should coordinate with for the wedding."

"Yours, of course," Grady says right away. "She's your mom."

Nico's shoulders tense. "She considers you her son, too."

"Yeah, but I'm not, really," Grady points out. *Like* a son and *actually* a son are two different things. He loves her, he knows she loves him, but their relationship isn't complicated and anchored with memories and a lifetime of love like an actual mother-son relationship. "Be honest: If she had to pick one of us, life or death situation, who would she pick?"

Nico crosses his arm and lifts his chin. "That's not a fair question. You and I both know she'd pick Lucas." Nico's belief that he's always second-best to his brother is more imagination and insecurity than reality. Amy goes on and on about both of them equally, and, if

Nico has to hear all about Lucas' accomplishments, then certainly Lucas gets an earful about Nico's. She's tremendously proud of her sons, *both* of them.

When Grady looks up, it's clear that Nico is prepared for a fight, but Grady just doesn't have the energy. "Just tell her to wear whatever she wants. Can we drop it?"

Nico's head tilts the other way, and his jaw works. He runs a hand through his hair and says, "No. All I do lately is drop it. I'm sorry if that makes me bossy or whatever, but enough."

Grady folds up his little paper, tucks the music in his pocket, and stands facing Nico. Today started so well, too. "Fine, then. Say what you need to." Maybe he's tired of hopping around and over things, maybe he needs to hear that everything has gone to shit and Nico has had enough, he's over it, because lord knows Grady is. Nico takes a breath, and Grady braces himself. "We should give her another chance," he says.

"What? Who?" This is not the conversation Grady was expecting. "You're not avoiding me because of the lawsuit and cameras and tabloids and everything?"

"Hmm? No." He flaps his hands. "Fuck those guys, I don't care. Lillian. Your mom? Not because you owe her anything, but because you owe yourself some closure, I want to hear her out."

Grady shakes his head; he doesn't understand. "Sweetheart, she left. That's what she does. There is nothing to hear out."

"You don't know that," Nico says. Grady's eyes helplessly track the exquisite line of his throat.

"You don't know *her*," Grady counters.

Nico's posture slumps, defeated. "That's because you won't let me. Look, I know she's a mess. And I know she's hurt you. But if my family is becoming your family like you said, then your family is becoming mine."

Grady's chest goes tight with warmth, with panic. He has no family to offer Nico, no mother to treat Nico like her own, no father to dole sage advice, no annoying brother to share, no extended family to warmly bring Nico into the fold. He has only abandonment and emptiness and heartbreak. "I'm just trying to protect you."

"I know." Nico's face softens; his body shifts into Grady's space. "And I appreciate it. But I'd like to remind you that my entire career was essentially helping hot messes get their lives together, or at least look together. I can handle her. I can handle all of it. Promise."

Grady looks at his feet and nods. He knows it's true, because Nico is the strongest, kindest, most determined person he's ever known, and it blows him away how capable he is. "You deal with so much for me already."

Nico hums, "That's true. And then you take your shirt off, and it's all worth it." Grady whips his head up, and Nico smirks.

"You're in it for the abs, then. I knew it." Grady holds his laughter, trying to look betrayed and not really selling it.

Nico replies with an indignant, "No." He adds, "Your ass is fantastic, too." Grady tilts Nico's chin up with a crooked finger, so he can put his lips on the warm pulse point of Nico's neck. "Oh, 'Abs and Ass,' there's your lullaby song title," Nico says, and Grady puffs a laugh against his skin.

"I love you," he murmurs.

"I love you, too," Nico says. "So we can give her one more chance? For me?"

Grady sucks the spot where his lips had been resting; he pulls at Nico's skin until his hands come up to grip Grady's hair and he gasps. "For you—" Grady says, pulling away to look at the darkening spot just below Nico's jaw. "Anything."

Nico's phone rings again, and, when Grady pulls away, Nico tilts it so Grady can't see the screen. "I should, uh—" He answers the phone with a terse, "Hello. Hold on." Then he strides into the bedroom and closes the door. Grady stares at the door in confusion. Nico's certainly allowed private phone calls, but that was strange. Curious now, Grady opens the laptop to see what Nico was hiding from him, but Nico returns too soon.

"Who was that?" Grady says, closing the laptop when Nico appears in the doorway.

"Oh." He makes weird face, a cross between and grimace and a smile. "Work. Stuff. Hey, you hungry? I'll scrounge up a late breakfast. I didn't really eat yet." And he's gone again, down the stairs, leaving Grady to follow, bewildered and worried. What is he up to?

23

Knoxville is three hours or so away, not far, but between Nashville and Knoxville is a whole lot of nothing. On tours when they have these long stretches of in-between, he'll sit by a window and knit or just watch the infinite stretch of highway. He's transient in those moments—not lonely, or meaningless, but outside of himself. No matter how good or bad things may be, the abiding truth of it is: *This too shall pass.* Today in Nico's car, as the hills start to become the Great Smoky Mountains on the horizon, the turmoil of their lives is outside of them for just a while, even where they're heading and why.

"You know what Dolly Parton did when she was having trouble with her record company?" Grady asks. They've just passed another billboard for Dollywood.

"Started a country music-themed amusement park?" Nico guesses.

"She actually dreamed her whole life about having her own amusement park."

Nico muses, "Don't we all," as he merges right for the approaching exit.

"She started her own label," Grady continues. "Course, the only person with the sort of leverage Dolly has is Dolly…"

"And maybe Clementine," Nico says.

Grady chuckles. "Yeah, maybe Clem."

Since it took Lillian an entire day to respond that she could meet with them that evening if they came to her, they decided to get a hotel for the night instead of driving back late—and likely disappointed. There are no five-star hotels in Knoxville, which doesn't bother Grady so much. He was poor for a long time; money and luxury don't mean a whole hell of a lot to him. It's nice and all, but he can cope without it.

"I'm just used to a certain lifestyle now," Nico says, half-joking and half-not, trailing his sleek suitcase behind him through the parking deck. "I bet if Stomp takes us for all we're worth, Clementine could let us use one of her houses, right?"

On the tip of his tongue is the reminder he keeps bringing up to Nico: that until they're married, it's only Grady who stands to lose everything; that it's not too late for Nico to get out. But Grady leaves it to sit unsaid and sour in his mouth; he doesn't want to talk about all that. They check in and go up to their room. It's nice enough; the hotel is decent. The downtown is small, but charming and laid-back busy in the way college towns tend to be. They eat a late dinner and wait, unpack for the night and wait. Grady watches TV, and Nico works on his tablet, and they wait.

"I'm gonna say it." Grady stretches his arms and yawns. If he sits on this couch much longer he's gonna conk out.

Nico frowns. "Let's give her a little longer to prove us wrong." Grady tips sideways onto the arm of the couch and pretends to fall asleep.

"Okay, fine. You were right; she's bailing." Nico says. Grady pretends to snore; Nico laughs and pinches his side. "Jackass."

And then, there's a knock on the door.

Nico rises to answer it when Grady doesn't, and from the couch in the corner Grady can hear her, though the open door blocks his view.

"I'm sorry I'm late. I— I was nervous, so I made banana bread, and it took longer than I remembered." Lillian laughs as Nico steps back so she can enter the hotel room. It's funny, Grady always expects her to look different, as if she's bigger and louder and brighter in his mind than she ever is in person. Next to Nico she looks so small, timid, and soft. Grady has to force his heart to harden against her.

"That why you took off last time? To make banana bread?"

She hangs her head, and Nico takes the foil-covered loaf from her hands to put it on the table by the window. He pulls one chair and then another over to the couch, setting them across the coffee table. "Why don't we..." Nico gestures at the chairs.

"Thank you for calling me," Lillian says to Grady. Her hands are clasped tightly in her lap; her right left jogs restlessly. Grady hates how much she looks like his Memaw and Granddaddy both; it unsettles him.

"It was Nico, not me."

She dips her head again. "All the same. I do appreciate it."

"What happened?" Nico asks, in his gentle-yet-no-nonsense way.

Lillian licks her lips and wrings her hands and says, whisper soft, "It's harder to break old patterns than I expected."

A silence stretches out uncomfortably. The hotel room is so quiet that when the air-conditioning kicks on it sounds like a sudden startling roar.

Lillian reaches for her purse, which is beside her chair, and sets it in her lap. "I brought some pictures." When she pulls a few photos out, Nico leans over eagerly. She places them on the table as she explains each one. "This is me and Mama and Daddy; I was about four here." Grady's seen that one before, or a similar one, the three of them on the front steps of the trailer: Memaw and Granddaddy with dark hair and faces round and smooth with youth, Lillian with two blond braids and a stuffed bunny tucked under one arm. Grady spent plenty of time poring over the photo albums and bins full of pictures when he was a little boy, trying to find a connection to this person he barely knew.

"And this is me and Vaughn and Grady. He was two, maybe?" This one Grady hasn't seen, and he doesn't remember taking it: It's the same set up as the previous picture, but with him in the center with wispy white-blond curls, Vaughn on one side, and Lillian on the other. Two-year-old Grady is grinning madly and clearly a half second away from bolting off the steps. "It was hard to keep him still long enough for a picture." Lillian laughs.

Grady's skin prickles with pins and needles, and his muscles go tense. He's jittery and irritated at her effort to claim him, as if she knew what he was like, as if she gets to laugh at the little boy that both of them left behind. "I wasn't the only one who wouldn't keep still," Grady says, the words bitter and biting.

Lillian's face falls, then twists angrily to match his. "Not like you made me feel welcome in your life, Grady. That's why I left before."

"Oh, it's my fault. Right, of course." His voice trembles with anger, and he has to look away, not at her, not at Nico who wants so badly for this to be something else but Grady can't— She found it right away, the raw wound that says it's his fault: He's too emotional, too energetic; he needs too much, wants to be loved so desperately that it's pushed her away, pushed everyone away, and it's only a matter of time before Grady and his life are too much for Nico, too. There is a *reason* he keeps his baggage locked up tight and shoved far, far down where he never has to look at it.

"Okay, hey, let's all take a breath." Nico is in diplomatic work-mode, in a star-having-a-temper-tantrum-on-the-red-carpet-mode. He moves to the couch, facing Lillian with his body twisted toward Grady. "I have the advantage of emotional distance here, so why don't I just—" He looks at Grady for consent to continue, which Grady gives with a glance and nod. "Lillian, you wanted to say something to Grady, and he wouldn't be here if he didn't want to hear you out. However, maybe he's earned the right to be wary, yes?" She nods several times, quickly and placatingly, no match for Nico's wily charms. "And Grady," He sets his folded hands beneath his chin, gives Grady his most serious-business arching eyebrow, and Grady doesn't even try to stop the resulting warm rush of adoration. "If you could dial back the furious resentment just a *skosh*, that would be super."

Despite himself, Grady's mouth lifts into a half-smile. "Fine."

Lillian crosses and uncrosses her legs, sets her wringing hands tightly between her knees, and opens her mouth several times to speak, then doesn't. She was sixteen when Grady was born, and he's always known that, but as she sits across from him still looking so young and lost, the lack of age separating them is more evident than ever. "I project when I'm feeling vulnerable," she finally offers. "It's a defense mechanism. It's not your fault I left. I was afraid and

I panicked and I left because that's what I always do." She looks from Nico to Grady. "I'm in therapy."

"Sounds like it's helping," Nico says. "And we're all here now, so let's try again."

Lillian blows a breath loudly through pursed lips, then presses them flat. "It was you—" She starts and Grady braces himself for another lash. "I'm sober, for the longest I've ever been. I got my GED and I have a job at a dental office and I'm even going to school to be a hygienist. I have my own place. I'm happy, really—finally. When Vaughn died, I thought, it'll be me next. And it wasn't just because I was afraid for myself, but because I thought of you and I couldn't be the next person who left you forever." Nico reaches for Grady's hand, gently unfolding his fingers. Grady is surprised to find that he's been clenching them. "I wanted you to know that I'm sorry and I'm trying and I wanted to be good enough for you. I hope it's not too late."

Grady doesn't know what to say, or if he can say anything. Nico speaks up, "Congratulations on getting sober and everything else you've accomplished. That's admirable."

"Thank you," she tells Nico, while her eyes dart to Grady. "You don't have to say anything. My therapist helped me see that I owe you an apology, but you don't owe me forgiveness. It's okay. That's— That's all I wanted to say."

Grady gathers the photos she brought, and for now that's all he can manage to accept from her. They look happy in the photo: Lillian and Vaughn and him in-between, as if for that snapshot in time they were happy.

"Were you two ever in love?" He's always wondered, would they have stayed in each other's lives if not for him? Did they resent their lifelong forced attachment because of him?

Lillian smiles, her eyes unfocused with a long-ago memory. "He was the cutest boy in school. All the girls wanted him, and he picked me. I couldn't believe it. *Me*. Vaughn was— so handsome and charming; it was like I was under a spell."

"I know exactly what you mean," Nico says, rubbing his thumb back and forth on the inside of Grady's wrist.

This time her smile is for the two of them tucked close on the couch. "We loved each other. Maybe not always the way we should have; I'm not gonna pretend things weren't bad, too. But a part of me never stopped believing we'd be a happy family someday." Her voice cracks on the last word, and she looks down to gather herself, clears her throat, and wipes her eyes. Lillian's grief for Vaughn must be at least as complicated as Grady's own feelings.

"I have his things, from Clay's house," Grady says, stopping to clear the tightness from his own throat. "Not with me, but next time you're in Nashville. If you wanna stop by…" It's the only offering he has for her.

"I'd like that very much." Her smile, this time, is only for him.

24

"**I miss hotels,**" Grady announces, bouncing on the end of the king-sized bed made up with snug hospital cornered sheets and about five times as many pillows as two people would ever need. Lillian left, and Grady made himself comfortable, stripping down to his underwear while Nico walked her out.

"Not me." Nico drops down beside him and unbuttons the cuffs on his shirt to fold up the sleeves. "This bed is too hard."

Grady lies back, wriggles up the firm mattress, and stretches out. "Remember the one we broke in New Orleans?"

"Oh, god, that was so embarrassing." Nico turns and moves up to his knees. His gaze roams up and down Grady's body as though he can't help himself. "What did you tell them when you checked out, anyway?"

Grady flashes a smoldering look at him when Nico finally looks at his face instead of everywhere else, making sure Nico knows that he noticed. "I told them my boyfriend was givin' it to me so hard we broke the bed," he says, then yanks Nico over top of him by the belt buckle.

"You ass, you did not." Nico arranges himself more comfortably; hovering on his hands and knees, then looks down at Grady with a dark look that's probably meant to be a rebuke, but is really just hot as hell. Grady leaves him to glower and busies himself unbuckling Nico's belt.

"I didn't tell 'em anything. They've dealt with worse than a cracked headboard, trust me." His own impromptu parties back in the day always got well out of hand. The belt jingles loose, and Grady moves on to the button and zipper of Nico's pants.

"Wait." Nico sits back, ass landing snugly on Grady's lap, and, despite Nico's stern look, Grady responds with a pleased groan. "How are you feeling? This whole meeting was kind of major. We should talk about it, probably."

Hotels are like the road, an in-between space. He fell in love with Nico in a hotel room, when it was just the two of them, where the rest of Grady's life didn't matter in that liminal space where anything was possible. "Don't wanna talk," Grady says. He pushes the flaps of Nico's pants open and the tucked in tail of his shirt falls to cover the front of his purple briefs; Grady slips his hand beneath and cups Nico where he's hot and well on his way to hard. "And I don't believe you really do either."

"We really sh—*shit*." Nico's head falls back, whatever he was saying lost as Grady curls his hand around the shape of him and jacks him through the thin fabric.

"What was that sweetheart? Didn't quite catch it," Grady says, squeezing tighter and rubbing faster; he does love getting a... *rise* out of Nico.

Nico's hips stutter, and he falls forward muttering, "Oh, fuck off," before crashing his mouth against Grady's. This is what he finds most intoxicating about Nico; peeling him loose of the buttoned-up, coolly imperious outer layer. How quickly he sheds the detachment needed to do his job and cope with the way Grady's public life bleeds into their private one. In bed with Grady, he's filthy and unhindered; his lips and hands demanding, his tongue curls wickedly. He wraps Grady around one little finger with only a whispered, "Don't move."

Grady doesn't. Not a muscle. He watches with heady anticipation as Nico gathers a towel and lube and condoms. Grady watches him toss the items down by Grady's hip, then methodically undress, fold his clothes and puts them in a neat pile on the couch, then stroke himself with a sideways grip on his cock that is meant to tease. "Hmm." His head tips from side to side as he surveys Grady on the bed as though he's an after-dinner treat; his dark eyes pin Grady to the bed. "How *do* I want you?"

He never has managed to work out how to not be so obvious about wanting to be consumed and wrecked and ravaged by Nico, so he doesn't hide his whimpers or the way his cock pushes hungrily against the y-front of his boxer briefs. Nico hums, very pleased. He perches on the bed, peels Grady's underwear off—finally, thank god—his tongue sweeps across his lips as Grady's cock falls heavily to his stomach.

"You are—" Nico starts, but whatever Grady is becomes lost in the hot slide of Nico's mouth greedily sinking down on Grady's cock. Nico looks up at him through his thick lashes. The sharp contours of his face are dramatic in the soft lamp light—cheeks hollowed and lips stretched—and Grady has never seen a prettier sight.

"Don't stop—" He blurts, then Nico pulls off so fast Grady's cock *pops* from his mouth, and Grady gasps from the sudden shocking loss. Whatever sense of propriety he had before, if any, he's lost now as Nico moves up Grady's body and settles languidly against the mound of pillows. Grady crawls after him, helpless as a moth to a flame. Grady finds his own reputation as a sex symbol ridiculous, though he's certainly pleased with the muscles he's sculpted and more than a little vain about his hair, and he is not *unaware* of the effect he has on people. But how anyone can look at the two of them and not be gobsmacked by Nico, who is gorgeous and sexy and commanding from his toes to the perfect swoop of his hair without any effort at all, Grady will never understand.

Grady turns words into poetry into music for a living and still all he can manage is, "Want you," when he spreads his knees wide over Nico's lap.

Then Nico is there, with one hand lifting his ass, then two blunt, slick fingers working Grady open. "I'm here," he says, and Grady kisses Nico's wet, open mouth as he relaxes into a yearning, aching emptiness.

Nico issues more commands: "Up. Not yet. Slow." And then Grady sinks down until Nico burns huge and full inside him, and neither of them has anything left to say at all. Grady rises slow, presses down slower, and rides Nico with his arms bent behind his head and his bottom lip pinched hard between his teeth. Nico's eyes look blown-black as he stares at the shift of Grady's thighs as he lifts and falls, at the straining lines of his abdominals, the knot of his biceps, the bob and sway of his hard cock. Grady certainly isn't shy, but only for Nico does he love being so decadently on display.

He can go for a quite a while like this; he's strong and fit, and vigorous sex beats squats and lunges any day. Grady can focus solely on Nico's pleasure, his hitching chest and dropped open mouth and guttural groans. He moves faster to make Nico swear and gasp, make his hips buck up and his hands grip bruises on Grady's hips. He moves slower to watch Nico fall gasping away from the edge and writhe with desperation beneath him. Faster and slow, more and less, until Nico touches him, and then it's all over. Grady comes helplessly, shuddering and hunched over and wheezing into Nico's shoulder. "Mmph," Grady says, wrung out and useless, as Nico flips them in a graceful arc.

Grady floats happily, giving his limp body for Nico to do as he pleases; Nico leans over so Grady's thighs are pushed back and out and slides back inside of him with one hard thrust, shocking Grady out of his floating, hazy bliss by hammering into him so hard the bed bangs against the wall. *There goes the headboard.* Grady wants to laugh, but Nico has a hand on Grady's over-sensitive, still-soft dick, then he experiments with the angle and strength of his thrusts until Grady jerks helplessly when he hits just the right spot and keeps on hitting it. Then Grady is hard again, coming again, weak spurts of it over Nico's hand, and they're both gasping for air as if they just swam up together from the bottom of the ocean.

Nico releases Grady's cock and grips the backs of his thighs with both hands, drives in and in and in, with his head tipped back and the sweat-sheen on his skin glowing gold from the lamplight, with dusky dark nipples and long lean muscles pulled tight, a gorgeous wrecked mess, and Grady needs to see him get off so badly. Grady rasps, his voice sex-slurred and rough as gravel. "Come on, gorgeous, let me see. Come for me, sweetheart." Nico pushes in once more, and his muscles lock up, a single cry spills from his throat, and Grady gets the extreme pleasure of watching Nico's face shatter into a beautiful ecstasy.

"How's the headboard?" Nico asks later. The room is dark and cool now even with their warm bodies tangled together. Grady reaches over his head. "Not broken," he confirms and puts his arm back around Nico's naked waist. Nico *hmms,* sounding a little disappointed, then says "That went really well, I think."

Grady nibbles on Nico's earlobe, because it's right there, and it's also early enough that he may be able to talk Nico into another attempt at breaking the headboard. "Well? I do believe you rocked my world once again."

"Not that," Nico says, wiggling closer and sighing happily when Grady drags the pointed tip of his tongue up to the shell of his ear. "Your mother."

"Oh." Grady pauses, head held awkwardly above his pillow. It went better than he expected, some of it anyway. Thing is, he's heard similar sentiments before. She's been sorry before, made promises before. The difference now is that Vaughn died, and she may well be all out of second chances. "We can invite her to the wedding, I guess. If you still want to."

Nico gives a little cheer, then drops a kiss on the knob of Grady's throat. She still might not show, in fact, the odds are good she won't, but he can give Nico this moment of victory. If he can't give her a chance for himself, he can do it for Nico.

"You know, with all the craziness lately…" Nico says, peppering kisses across Grady's chest. "I'm not going anywhere, I, I know I've had my moments of not handling things well, but— You do know that I'm here. Right?"

The rest of the world can only be held off for so long, that's the problem with transitional places like the road and hotels and stages. They go away, and everything else doesn't. Grady recalls the secret phone call, the things hidden on Nico's computer screen he clearly didn't want Grady to see. He remembers the lawsuit and the counter lawsuit and the threat of losing everything hanging over them, that he is stuck, but Nico isn't, not really. He is here, but should he be?

"Sure," Grady says and he kisses Nico and slides their bodies together and makes them both forget for a little while longer.

The banana bread that Lillian brought smells delicious, and Grady doesn't have to taste it to know that it's his Memaw's recipe. He puts it in the back seat and drops the pictures on top; the one of her and Vaughn and Grady slips down to the seat. He does look like him, Vaughn. His father. He's not *like* Vaughn, no. If it wasn't for Memaw and it wasn't for music he would have *been* Vaughn—same life, same mistakes, same ending. Even with his grandparents and his music as a saving grace, he almost was Vaughn anyway, and no matter how deep down and packed away, part of him will always be that person. Now here it is, dragged out into the daylight again for everyone to see.

"So there's bad news and less bad news."

Yang, Zorn, and Howard: Celebrity and Creative Law Associates is one block from the "Mother Church" of country music, the Ryman Auditorium, and two blocks from the river. The law office is in a red-brick building on a block of red-brick buildings and red-brick sidewalks. The rugs are burgundy, and the furniture is all shining mahogany and dark leather. They're on the fifth floor, yet it's as if Grady is in a dark red subterranean cave. Nico and Gwen's office isn't too far away, but Grady is just at the lawyer's office to get briefed about how the preliminary hearing with Stomp Records went, so he told Nico not to bother coming.

"Less bad news first, I reckon," Grady says.

Tanisha Howard is a powerful name in the industry; she's gone to bat for many artists over the years and won, but in person she's soft-spoken with a wide, sweet smile, is pretty and young, and wears shiny silk shirts with bows and gold broaches shaped like butterflies. Her opponents probably underestimate her every single time.

"An optimist. I can appreciate that," Tanisha says, with her big, friendly smile. Going forward—if there is a forward—Grady would be happy to keep her on his team permanently. He does quite like Ms. Tanisha Howard, Attorney at Law, even if she is bringing him bad and worse news. "Stomp Records is not budging on either the breach of contract claim, or the lack of contract fulfillment assertion," she says in one breath.

Grady rubs at his chin that's itchy with a few days' stubble. "That's the good news?"

"The *less bad* news," she corrects. Grady twirls his hand in a "go on" gesture and she adds, "The bad news is, they've filed another claim, stating that your contract is now void and you are obligated to restart the seven-year exclusivity agreement as well as produce three additional albums within the confines previously agreed upon in the violated contract."

Grady furrows his brows and squints one eye and chews on that. "You gotta be kiddin' me," he says.

"There are two things I don't do, Mr. Dawson." Ms. Howard closes the file folder on her desk and folds her hands on top of it. "Kid anyone and lose cases. Don't give up hope; I certainly haven't."

It's not hope that's the problem. Grady's always had that in abundance; he's had to. It's the ultimate betrayal of the thing that saved him, of music, his music, being what could now bring him down for good. Grady knows exactly who he is without music.

On his way to his truck Grady is greeted by cameras; this part of downtown is prime for celebrity pickings. He keeps his head down and pushes through; he doesn't care what he looks like or what they shout at him or what salacious lie will be published about him. He drives to Nico and Gwen's studio because he promised he would.

To his surprise, it's Spencer who greets him. Gwen is busy working at her desk, and Nico is talking to a man with slicked-back blond hair wearing an ill-fitting polyester suit. If he's a client, he is not taking Nico's style expertise under advisement.

"Hey, Grady, look. You were totally right about flipping off the paps." Gwen turns her computer screen so he can see; it's a picture of them in the car. And below that, one of him and Nico on their way to Knoxville. "Oh, yeah," Gwen says, when he frowns at the second one. "Everyone is all abuzz about where you were going and if you're still together. And they were just starting to lose interest, too."

Grady moves the screen away. "Great."

"Don't worry," Spencer calls from the reception desk. "I've gotten them completely off the trail of your wedding. They all think it's been cancelled." Grady doesn't have the emotional reserves to tell him that it just might be. Spencer grins and adjusts his glasses. "I've been using the name Ocin Ydarg. Get it?"

Gwen answers him first, "Spencer, that is the worst fake name of all time."

Spencer stands in challenge. "I'd like to see you do better." Then Gwen stands, too, and they spend the next several minutes coming up with louder and more random combinations of Nico and Grady's names, until Nico's meeting is finished and the blond guy in the cheap baggy suit leaves. "Nico, what's your middle name?" Spencer asks, after Nico closes the office door.

"I don't have one." He holds Grady's elbow and kisses his cheek; he looks amazing today, and smells incredible, and Grady's stomach goes tight. "How was your briefing?"

"Bad. What was that about?" He recognizes the churn in his gut; he's suspicious. Something about that guy and the secretive way they were talking and the side glances in Grady's direction have raised his hackles. He's early. He was supposed to meet Nico after lunch. "Who was that?"

"Oh." Nico blinks too fast, then steps back. "Maintenance guy. There's uh. Plumbing." He gestures vaguely to the ceiling. He walks away before Grady can ask what sort of plumbing problems they could be having in the ceiling, and Spencer pipes up again. "Grady, what's your middle name?"

Grady doesn't answer. He follows Nico to ask again who that guy really was, then he spots a business card on Nico's desk with blond guy's face on it. He slips it into his pocket when Nico isn't looking. "Vaughn," he finally answers Spencer. "My middle name is Vaughn."

When he's back at home by himself, Grady goes right to the office, where he sways back and forth in the office chair picking at a corner of the business card with his thumb. The guy's name is Chet. He's a real estate agent, and Grady can't decide if he's Nico's type because Nico's type before Grady was decidedly not-Grady: serious, mature men with serious mature jobs that didn't come with paparazzi camped outside of their houses or fans digging up his personal business or record companies asking him to hide his relationship. Grady types Chet's name and waits for the search results to load. He's tense with brittle jealousy, and he hates— Why can't he just temper his emotions? Why can't he feel things in a *reasonable* way? Why is he so much?

Chet sells rural properties, retail spaces mostly, some land available for development. His "about" page says that he and his wife Jessica have two kids: Brylie and Chasen.

Reasonable, rational: Maybe Nico is looking for a bigger office space, maybe they're looking to expand. Why rural he doesn't know—for storage? Grady goes down to the garage, trying to get a grip on his cyclone of thoughts. *Don't lose hope. It was for you. You look just like him. Just one more person who left you.* He rips out upholstery and engine parts, busted lights and rusted handles. The car was abandoned, left to rust and rot. Grady has two options: strip it bare and start all over, or painstakingly replace broken bit by broken bit and hope it may someday slowly come back to life.

He's dripping with sweat and dizzy from the stifling heat in the garage. He takes his shirt off and uses it to wipe his face and neck and leans over the open hood of the car to catch his breath, slow his thoughts, take the dangling, frayed ends of his life and figure out how to pull his way back up again without music and with Nico and so many other people counting on him, believing in him, wanting things from him—

His phone rings with Amy's ringtone: "If Mama Ain't Happy."

He fumbles the phone in his grimy, sweaty hands, then presses it to his ear to hear, "Great news, the snapdragons came in after all."

Grady props himself on the edge of the hood. "I'm glad. Only had to give 'em a little more time, right?" He sounds breathless to his own ears. Amy picks up on his rough voice right away. "What's the matter, my darling?" That's all it takes, her kind, motherly tone. He breaks, sobbing like a little boy over the phone to his maybe, hoped-for future-mother-in-law.

26

Grady busies himself under the car, which he's put up on blocks. He's removed the flat, worn-out tires, the shredded brake pads, and the cracked fuel tank. All of those parts should be easy enough to replace. His life is another story entirely, but it's fine, he's fine. As long as he's focused on the car, he's fine, even if a little embarrassed over his breakdown. He's relieved and somewhat unburdened; he didn't know how badly he needed to get that all out until it kinda just… did. One end of the fuel tank comes loose, and Grady pushes his heels against the concrete floor and scoots the wheeled creeper over to work on the other end.

"I hear Roy Orbison, so I know you're in here somewhere." Grady rolls himself out on the creeper to find Nico standing over him. Before Grady sits up, Nico slowly takes in Grady's torn-up jeans, grease-stained arms, the smears across his bare chest, the hair clumped with sweat and he remarks, "I may have to reconsider my stance on disliking this car."

Of course, Nico would have a thing for the greasy mechanic look. Grady heaves himself up and mops his face and neck with his shirt. "How late is it?"

Nico winces. "Late, sorry."

"Lots of late nights, huh?"

It's there, whatever he's hiding, fighting to be said in the struggle in Nico's eyes and the firm set of his mouth, as if he's barely keeping it contained behind his tightened lips. Nico darts his gaze away to the steel workbench. "What's that? Transmission?"

Grady follows the conversational detour, for now. The Superbird's transmission is laid out in puzzle pieces: the dozen or so parts Grady has disassembled, cleaned and greased, ready to be reassembled. "Yeah, it's not in bad shape. Needs some new seals, maybe a gasket, but I'm optimistic I can rebuild it."

Nico's look back at him is soft, warmly loving, and it's so hard for Grady to have any fight left when Nico looks at him like that. Grady loves him, but, more than that, he has to find a way to trust that Nico means it when he says he loves Grady. Grady stops the music blasting from his old boom box, closes the hood of the car, and covers the transmission parts with a tarp. "Your mom is coming here."

Nico narrows his eyes, and his head slowly tips to the right. "At the end of next month for the wedding, you mean."

"Um," Grady says, his voice sliding up. "No. Tomorrow night. We were talking and— I guess she sorted out that I was havin' a hard time lately."

Nico's head un-tilts, but his face is unreadable. Sad? Tired? Hiding? "Yeah, she's good at that." He pulls his phone from his pocket and scrolls through a long line of text messages; his eyebrows lower and rise several times over. He pockets it and announces,

"Okay, I'll send a car to the airport for them. Dad's coming, too." Then he untucks his shirt and uses it to fan his stomach. "As much as I'm enjoying the sweaty, shirtless view, it's like the inside of a steamer basket in here."

Grady agrees. The setting of the sun hours ago had little effect on the stifling, moist heat; it's fall now, technically, but the summer weather won't release them from its grip for weeks. As soon as they step inside, Grady's skin prickles with goosebumps. The punishing heat outside is cathartic much like singing or playing guitar or sex or going for a long run: the release that drugs or alcohol used to be. Nico's solid, sure presence and the air-conditioning inside are a blessed relief; he can only stew in his own toxins for so long.

"Go shower, and I'll order some food," Nico says, pausing in the kitchen to set down his bag and unload his pockets. Before he goes, Grady pecks Nico's cheek; there's a hint of stubbled roughness against his own. Nico always clean-shaves every morning. He must be stressed out, too. How could he not be? Is he looking for an exit strategy of some sort, a delay or an option B if he's foolishly determined to not leave altogether? "Hey." Nico catches Grady's hand as he moves away. "I know things are hard right now, but we will get through it. Hang in there."

"I'm trying to," Grady says. Lord, is he trying. "I don't know what else to do."

Nico releases him with a wide-eyed look of warning. "Well, sounds like help is on her way direct from Sacramento."

Grady gets up early the next day and mows their sloping front and side lawns instead of going for a run, has Flora drop by with some mums for their garden, plants them among the tall yellow goldenrods and dainty orange helenium flowers and the fuzzy clumps of lamb's ear that Cayo likes to pet with one pointed chubby finger when he isn't toddling off or picking flowers or throwing rocks. The leaves on the two juneberry bushes he and Nico and Flora planted in the garden in memoriam for Grady's grandparents are showing the first hints of the brilliant red they'll be once cool weather finally arrives.

After that, he sees Nico off and spends the rest of the day cleaning the house from top to bottom. That song comes back to him as he's sweeping; the lullaby picks up tempo, goes from wistful and solemn to an angry undertone, an old anger that Grady knows all too well, a cadence he's heard for a long time, notes and words he's been collecting his whole life. He abandons the broom and a pile of dirt and debris on the kitchen floor to scribble down the music and lyrics before he can shove them away again. Emotionally wrung out, he goes on another run to drain the tension physically, too.

He circles back to finish cleaning, cleans himself, and sits down to knit to keep his still-anxious hands busy—a good anxious now, an excited anxious, until his phone vibrates with the message he's been waiting for.

Nico: Plane is arriving on time. I'll try to beat them home.

Grady finishes three and a half fingerless gloves for the cooler months—assuming they will eventually arrive—when he hears car doors slamming closed. He jumps up to greet them on the porch. "Mr. Takahashi, sir." Grady shakes Ken's wide, solid hand and grabs his sturdy shoulder with the other. He's like a broader, grayer, more stoic version of Nico. "And Amy." He bends to scoop her up in a hug—he's been expressly forbidden to call her Mrs. Takahashi.

"Oh, let me look at you, it's been too long." She squeezes Grady's face between both of her hands after he sets her back down on the porch. "So handsome. Ken, look how handsome!"

"Yes, very handsome." Nico's dad looks at the luggage the driver brought up. "Where can I take these bags?"

Grady insists on carrying most of the suitcases himself, though Ken grabs two, then Grady gets them settled in the guest room at the far end of the top floor. It has a nicer view of the woods behind their house than the downstairs one, and it has Nico's old bed and funky refinished vintage dresser and shelves. "The bathroom is the first door on the left," Grady says, when Nico arrives to join them.

Nico gets a handshake and back pat from his dad and a hug from his mom that he crouches for. "I've missed you, my handsome boys," she says, patting Nico's cheek, then his chest, and frowns as she asks, "What is this shirt, Nico? So bright."

Nico looks down at it with pouted lips. "Neon is on-trend again," he says, more to himself than her. His shirt is neon stripes with neon triangles, and on anyone else it wouldn't work at all. But it's Nico, so, of course, it does.

"I like it," Grady says.

Nico replies, with great emphasis, "Thank you, *Grady*."

"Okay," Amy says, hauling a suitcase half her size onto the bed, and then a slightly smaller one after that. Ken is unpacking clothes into the dresser and setting his toiletries on top, as quiet as Amy is chatty. "Nico, I brought you those seaweed crisps you like from Costco." She unzips the smaller bag. It's completely filled with boxes of roasted and salted seaweed chips. Nico gasps and grabs one of the boxes.

"Thanks, mom, you're the best."

"You know we do have a Costco here," Grady points out.

Nico replies with disdain and a mouthful of seaweed snacks, "As if I'm going to shop at Costco. Grady, please."

"And Grady," Amy says, opening the other suitcase. "I couldn't remember if you liked plain M&M's or peanut more, and they also had the white chocolate Kit Kat bars I know are your favorite, only in a variety pack, so I hope you like Reese's Cups and Hershey Bars, too." She pulls out a pound-size bag each of both plain and peanut M&M's, and a bulk pack of thirty full-size candy bars. "Oh, I hope they didn't melt."

Grady is speechless, overwhelmed that she thought of him and remembered his favorite candy and then went to the trouble of hauling a suitcase full of it all the way across the country.

"I dunno, Mom, maybe you should have gotten sixty candy bars," Nico says, loudly crunching on his seaweed snacks. "That's not nearly enough junk food."

Amy furrows her brows and pats one of the extra-large bags of M&M's. "Oh, no."

"He's joking, dear," Ken says, in a flat tone. He gathers his bathroom items and heads off down the hall.

"Nicolas," she chides, swatting at Nico. Grady chuckles and thanks her, then reassures her that it's more than enough and he very much appreciates it. "Oh," she says, digging around in the bigger suitcase again. She pulls out a raincoat, a mesh ball cap, nylon waterproof pants, and socks that say *MAXDRY* on the store tag. "I was at the new garden center on Winslow. Nico, you remember where that video store used to be when you were little—"

"No, I do not," Nico says.

She continues, ignoring him, "I think it's a flooring place now? Next to that they opened a garden center, and next to *that* I saw there was a running store, and the woman who works there said all this stuff is good for running in the rain. I was telling her about how my sons are in Nashville, and how much it rains here with the thunderstorms, and I worry, Grady, about you running in the rain without proper gear."

Grady wants to scoop her up in another hug and never let go; he could not possibly love this woman more. "Thank you," he says, clutching the rain pants and coat and hat and socks to his chest, tight against his full, happy heart. "This is— Thank you." He swallows and sniffs, and she seems to understand that his gratitude is for more than the rain gear and candy.

She reaches up to cradle his face in her hands. "Of course, my darling."

27

Grady has so many memories of Memaw; a hope chest full of her laugh and her smile and her cooking and her kisses dropped on the crown of his head. Memaw was everything good and warm and kind in this world, and if Grady is ever even close to being as kind or warm or good, it's because of her. He tries and fails and tries again, because she believed that he could. So he does. He falls, he gets up, he falls. She'd make him brownies and kiss the messy curls on his head and say, *It's okay, angel. Failing just means you get to try again.*

When he wakes to the smell of pancakes, his still-sleepy mind takes him to a Saturday morning in the trailer, waking to find Memaw in the kitchen and Granddaddy in his chair and Johnny Cash singing a hymn on the radio. *Keep my feet from wandering. There from thee I'll roam. Lest I fall upon the wayside. Lead me gently home.*

"Mornin' angel," she'd say. "Go on, set the table, now."

The confusion clears from Grady's head, and he sits up in his house not in the rural shadowed outskirts of Nashville, but on a hill that overlooks its skyline.

Nico is up early and gone again; the rare days that he does so are becoming less and less rare. Grady throws some clothes on and goes down to find Ken watching TV in the living room and Amy in the kitchen. She sets a plate of pancakes in front of him and informs him that Nico didn't eat anything at all.

"In your freezer you have banana bread and ice cream and in your refrigerator you have milk, soda, ketchup, and blackberry jam. Lucky I found pancake mix in the cabinet. Where is your food? What do you eat?"

Grady spreads jam on his pancakes and sits at the breakfast bar. "We get takeout," he says, deciding not to mention that Nico lives mostly on a diet of green smoothies, protein bars, and black coffee and the longer Grady lives with him the more he does, too, plus, Mello Yello. "Been kinda hard for us to get to the store, even more than usual," Grady admits.

She makes the same tight-lipped disapproving face that Nico so often does. "I saw those cameramen outside. Shameful."

Grady eats his pancakes and nods. "I try to remind myself that people are just curious and don't mean any harm. I know it bothers Nico a whole lot, though."

Amy gets the milk from the fridge, pours a glass, and puts that down on the breakfast bar for him, too. It's really only there for the days Nico doesn't take his coffee black, but Grady drinks it without a word of complaint.

"Nico is very strong-willed," she says. "He can handle it." Grady laughs a little at the understatement. *Strong-willed*, yes indeed. "I'll have him stop at the market." Amy pulls a notepad and pen from her purse and starts a list. "He said he was running errands today."

Grady is unaware of any errands needed, but he has been stuck in the bubble of this house as his career crashes around him. Later in the day, Grady gives Amy and Ken a more detailed tour of the house. They stop in the garage when Ken expresses interest in the Superbird.

"It's not a complete lost cause," he declares, which seems like high praise to Grady. "How did you learn to fix cars? Self-taught?"

The hood of the car clangs loudly closed in the humid garage. "Ah, my grandfather's old Cadillac was always breaking down. I learned how to replace a hose, rig a starter, and jump a dead battery before I could crawl."

Ken gives him a solid pat on the back. "You'll fix it, then," he says, with total confidence. Grady glows with pride.

After lunch Ken decides to take a nap, and Amy isn't any better at sitting still for more than a minute than Grady is, so they take a walk in the woods. The heat hasn't backed down any; even the wind is hot. But Amy marches along at a quick pace, decked out in a tennis dress with a pink sun visor and matching pink fanny pack.

"So, what are your options?" She slows her pace a little as they talk about his legal troubles.

"Well, I can agree to what they want: a new song, or maybe a whole new album. Start all over with my contract, we're talking several years of commitment, best-case scenario. Worst-case scenario is they refuse every album, and I'm stuck in limbo for good." Grady jumps to avoid a muddy patch; it must have rained a bit last night. "Or I can keep fighting them and risk losing a whole lot of money and everything I've worked for and bring Nico down with me. That's why it's just too much, carrying on with the wedding and all."

They reach the end of the dirt trail, where it connects to a paved pathway that's busy with bikes and joggers and people walking dogs. "And Nico wants to fight them and keep the wedding on track," Amy says. They've talked about that plenty, and Nico has probably discussed it with her, too. "What about what *you* want to do?"

Grady is lost in thought as they walk back, because he hasn't much considered what he wants. He's been so worried about what Nico wants and what the label wants and what his fans want and— No, he does know. "I just want to make music," he finally decides.

Amy looks up at him sternly, a mom-look if he's ever seen one, "Then make music. Nobody gets to take that from you. That's in here, that's yours." She stops to poke at his chest, over his heart. Then she unzips her fanny pack. "I brought protein bars and water, if you need it."

He takes one of each; he really did need it, as it turns out.

Back at the house, Amy goes upstairs, and Grady heads down, texting Nico: *Pick up chicken thighs and ingredients for a tare sauce, she says you know. And eggplants and mushrooms and honeydew melon. And why don't we have skewers? And be home soon.*

He texts back when Grady is settled in the studio and is already at work with his guitar and a notebook and with a pencil set in his teeth.

Nico: Ok. We do have skewers. Somewhere. I don't know the ingredients for tare but Google does. BTW now who's bossy?

And because Grady can never resist flirting a little he sends: *still you ;)*

His first memory of Memaw is her singing him to sleep. He doesn't know how old he was, but he remembers being in the twin-size bed that was Lillian's and became his the more time he spent there and the less she did. It was something Memaw did a thousand times: sit on his bed and rub his back and sing to him in the dark until he finally gave in to sleep. In this memory, she says the words she said hundreds of times, words he believed and then didn't, wouldn't believe again until it was too late to tell her that he knew and he felt the same way.

Goodnight, angel. Do you know special you are? You are so special to me.

He doesn't know why that night sticks out in his mind's eye; if something else significant happened that day it's lost to time now. It's always been a comfort to him, though, just like music is. So he starts with that memory, and begins to write.

Would you sing me one more lullaby?
In the dust of your taillights.
Tell me the story of the man you shoulda been
Words in cracked windshields sayin' this is why you ran
Mama, Daddy
Sing me one more lullaby before you go.

When Grady finishes the song, he's surprised to see the sun setting, and when he emerges from the studio he sees that Nico came home; his keys and wallet are in the copper dish and the mail's been dropped on the counter. Grady finds everyone gathered on the patio sitting on benches surrounding the cold fire pit.

"There he is! We were under strict orders to not bother you," Amy says.

"Oh, yeah, sorry. I get a little lost in my head when I'm writing a song." There's food prepped on a tray next to the grill; meat and mushrooms and chopped eggplants on skewers and brushed with a dark sauce, corn wrapped in foil, melon cut into triangle slices. "Y'all didn't have to wait for me."

Ken picks up the plate of meat and motions for Grady to follow him with the corn. "We didn't fly all the way out here to eat family dinner without you."

The grill is hot, and Grady stands by with the tongs while Ken slides the food onto the grate. "Nice grill," he says. It's the highest of manly compliments.

"It's the only type of cooking I know how to do, so I figured I oughta do it right."

Ken nods wisely. "A good choice." And then asks, bluntly and without segue. "Why are you thinking of postponing the wedding?"

"Oh." Grady pushes the sizzling skewers around, just to give himself time to change topics. "It's— There's a lot going on. I don't want Nico to have to deal with so much at once. I don't know long *I'll* be dealing with it. May be a long, long time."

"You're giving him an out, if he doesn't really want to go through with it. Is that right?"

Grady can't deny it, not to that stern face. "Yes, sir. I suppose that's true."

And then it's quiet again, save for the noise of the food cooking and the cicadas' unceasing buzz in the trees. Grady checks the meat, turns the corn. Then Ken speaks again. "I've been married for almost thirty-seven years now and what I know for certain is that it's a complete crapshoot." Grady nearly drop the tongs right onto the ground; he has no clue how to respond to that. "And I also know," Ken continues, "that if you find someone who is willing to hang on through all the crap, you don't let go of them. Now, I've known my son longer than you have, but I'd say you're a little closer to him these days." Ken turns a no-nonsense look on Grady. "Have you ever known Nico to do anything he doesn't really want to do?"

A grin tugs at Grady's mouth. "No sir, I can't say that I have."

"Mmhmm," Ken replies. He nods at the grill. "Better go ahead and flip those, they're ready."

28

The second to last day of the visit starts with waffles and Nico announcing that he's taking Amy and Ken to all the tourist stops in Nashville: The Country Music Hall of Fame, The Ryman Auditorium, The Parthenon, Cheekwood Botanical Gardens, and, if they have time, the art museum. Worried he'll attract too much attention and ruin the day, Grady declines to go, despite Ken and Amy's protests. He's itching to get the new song laid down on something other than his primitive recording equipment, so, once they all leave, he sends a message to Clem: *Can you find me some studio time?*

Clem: Gimme a couple hours.

Ten minutes later she texts again.

Clem: Okay, I got it.

The address she sends him is up in north Nashville in an area with storage facilities and big warehouses, and the studio itself is tucked away in a massive gray concrete building. "These places get more random every time," Grady comments when he finds her waiting at the front door spinning a key ring around one finger.

"You ever hear the phrase 'beggars can't be choosers,' Mr. Dawson?" She slides the key in and shoves the door open with a hard jut of her hip. Despite the rough outward appearance, the studio inside is done up very nicely, with brand-new equipment and state-of-the-art boards; the booth is outfitted with top-notch soundproof panels.

"This place is great, Clem. Thanks." He sets his guitar case on the black leather couch and flips the latches open. "How do you find these studios?"

"A magician never reveals her secrets," Clem says. She sits at one of the high-backed chairs at the soundboard. "You know, I've been worried about you giving up on all this."

The strings squeak beneath his fingers as he lifts the guitar from the case. "I thought about it," he confides. "I thought maybe I'd have to give it up. Be a music teacher or take up handyman work to pay the bills. I dunno. Wouldn't be so bad, would it?" He strums a few chords to check the tuning. It never stops being something of a miracle, even now, making music with his own hands, creating something that didn't exist before, and if only he hears it or if it hits number one on the radio doesn't really matter much. It still exists; it's still music, and he still has something that no one can take away from him.

"I'd give you a month before you found yourself on a stage again. And that's being generous." Clem flips her cascading golden hair over her shoulder and starts to bring the soundboard to life. "By the way," Clem says, "I have another magical surprise up my sleeve for you."

Then, as if indeed by magic, the door opens and four familiar people make their raucous way into the studio. "Grady! My man!"

The backing band he's had on his last two tours and all three albums surrounds him: Brad, the seasoned silver-haired drummer; Mongo, the giant teddy bear bassist; skinny loud-mouthed Billy on banjo; and Mandy, fiddle player and saint who puts up with all of them. They're all free agents, so they aren't his exclusively, though nothing bonds a group of people like living on a bus together and spending months making music while crammed in tight spaces for hours and days at a time.

"Sorry to hear about all your troubles," Brad says. "Wish I could help somehow."

"Buncha crooks," Billy adds.

"It's all right," Grady reassures them. "I'm here still, ain't I?"

Mongo slings a huge arm over Grady's shoulders and tugs him against his side. "A little lawsuit won't get our Grady down, no, sir."

"Forget about all that," Mandy says, getting her fiddle out and starting to tune it. "Congrats on the engagement!"

Billy and Mongo chime in with their congratulations, and Billy says, "The lone wolf has been leashed. Listen, Grady. I have a speech for the reception all set—" He props his elbows on the top of his banjo case and pretends to be holding a microphone. "I'll never forget the night I met Grady, or the women we took ho—"

He's interrupted by a sharp jab to his ribs from Mandy followed by a glare that makes him snap his mouth shut. "What is wrong with you?"

Grady grins anyway; he's just so happy to be here with these guys. "Maybe keep working on that speech, and, for now, how about we make some music?"

The day passes quickly, and by evening Grady has vocals and his lead guitar track laid down, as well as some of the band's tracks and a backing vocal appearance from Clementine on the chorus. The mix is basic, quickly done and not ready for anyone else to hear. Grady's really got something here, though, rough as it is. The band leaves, and then it's him and Clem at the boards, putting final touches on the recording.

"Thanks again," Grady says. "I don't know why you do all this stuff for me, but I really do appreciate it."

"Grady." She turns her chair to give him one of her calculating stares. "You know why I decided to help you build your career?"

Grady turns his chair, too. "Hmm. It's a strange hobby of yours?"

She smiles and shakes her head. "No. Because I saw something special in you. And I knew that you had what it takes. I still do. What is the point of having success, if I don't use to it pull other people up and give them a chance, too?"

She may be mysterious and take-no-prisoners, suffer-no-fools driven, but, "You're good people, Clementine Campbell." He kisses the top of her head, and she leans her cheek on his shoulder.

"You know this is why people think we're dating, right?"

Grady nuzzles against her silky hair. "Nah, it's because we make beautiful music together."

Clementine *tsks*; a laugh puffs into Grady's neck. "I know you know exactly how that sounds, mister." They listen to the last few stanzas of the rough-cut song while the download finishes, then Clementine asks in an unusually trepidatious voice, "You gonna be okay?"

He always is, somehow; by crook or by hook, he'll manage. "Yeah, darlin', I'll be okay."

It's dark when he gets back to the house. He didn't plan to be so late and he regrets that he missed dinner with the family. The place is dark and quiet; seems he missed them altogether. The guest bedroom door is closed; the light inside is turned off. There is a light coming from the crack below their office door, so Grady opens it a sliver to let Nico know he's home.

"No, I need to cancel it completely." Nico is on his phone, at the desk with his back to the door, dressed as if he was on his way to bed in a snug gray T-shirt and thin linen pants, so soft and beautiful that Grady wants to curl up against him and touch him everywhere. Grady moves to close the door and wait for him in bed as a surprise, when Nico says into the phone, "The venue is wonderful, no, it's not that. We're just cancelling the wedding. Well, thank you for the condolences but that's not— Yes, I understand the deposit is nonrefundable."

Somehow Grady moves from the door, somehow his feet carry him to the bed, somehow he gets undressed and under the covers and stays perfectly still with his eyes closed when Nico comes to bed and turns on his side facing away from Grady. And then all he can hear is his own panicked breathing and the frantic pump of blood through his aching heart.

Grady was right; Nico did want out. He was right, too, that he'd have to choose in the end, Nico or his career, and now it's too late—he's losing both. This is what he's been sneaking around about then, but why didn't he say? Why not take the outs that Grady offered to him instead of telling him to hang in there and that he's not going anywhere? Grady flew too close to the sun again, let himself believe that everything was bright and beautiful and he couldn't get burned, not again, not this time, not with Nico, no. He's different. He was different, Grady really thought— Why does he never, ever see it coming?

29

Grady Dawson Gets Real About Doing Things His Own Way
by Hannah Jordan

It seems as if controversy follows Grady Dawson around like a hound dog in a clichéd country song, but for a guy who can't seem to keep his name out of the tabloids, he is remarkably laid-back. On a hot late summer day out on the covered porch of his Nashville hills home with that trademark half-cocked grin, Grady greeted me with a hearty handshake, requested that I remove my shoes if I don't terribly mind, then invited me in for iced tea and banana bread.

While he was in the midst of dealing with a breach-of-contract lawsuit by his label, Stomp Records, a countersuit, and an upcoming day in court, I sat down with Grady not long after the news first broke to discuss his career, his personal life, and what he hopes will happen moving forward.

ENN: I know you can't legally discuss the details of the lawsuits, but what, for you, has been the most difficult part?

Grady Dawson: *At first it was the waiting around, not knowing what would happen, like I'd just hit this huge, impossible roadblock after working so hard. But the worst part really was not being able to make music, like I wasn't allowed to.*

ENN: Would you say you're bitter about what went down?

Grady Dawson: *The thing about country music as an industry is that it is a business. I've never really wanted to mess around with that whole side of things, which is partly why I'm dealing with all of this now. A contract is a contract. I do understand that much; I understand the record company has a lot at stake as well. To my mind, I met my obligations. I gave them an album; I fulfilled that contract. I'm not bitter. I'm disappointed more than anything.*

ENN: Can you tell us about the album?

Grady Dawson: *It's very personal, even more so than my first two albums. The people on the business side of music maybe don't quite understand what it takes out of you to bare your soul on a music track, but I do it because that's my church, that's my salvation, and I always hope that anyone listening might connect to that and take a little bit of comfort for their own struggles or know that someone else is celebrating their triumphs along with them. I didn't set out to be controversial; I just wanted to be honest.*

ENN: This is isn't the first time you've had disagreements with Stomp, but has it gone this far before?

Grady Dawson: *No. The thing is, I'm grateful to Stomp Records for signing me and for standing by me when I was determined to keep* *making mistakes until I hit rock bottom. They weren't often happy with my behavior, and for good reason. That's why [the lawsuit] is so upsetting; I never expected the point of no return to be me falling in love, finally being happy and at peace, and just wanting to share that with everyone who has shown me so much love and support over the years.*

ENN: So let's get the official word, instead of Internet rumors. You are engaged.
Grady Dawson: Yes.

ENN: Why not talk about it?
Grady Dawson: I want to be really, really clear on this: I am not ashamed of my relationship with [stylist fiancé] Nico and I am not hiding it. In fact, it's been important to both of us to be open and visible and proud, but to still maintain some privacy. It's a hard balance. We wanted a quiet, simple, private wedding, and then we would share the news with everyone. The point was to avoid rumors and speculation, which we obviously did not succeed at. It is what it is, though.

ENN: Nico is here, but declined to be interviewed. So I'm just going to say this because I know I'll get a ton of messages about it: Yes, he is very sharply dressed.
Grady Dawson: [Laughs] Always. Even his pajamas are designer.

ENN: You two met when he styled you for a photoshoot—the infamous surprise haircut photoshoot—has it been difficult for him to go from being behind the cameras, so to speak, to now being pictured on the cover of gossip magazines?
Grady Dawson: It has. I think even more so for him because he's seen this all go down from the sidelines, so he understands it intimately.

It's why we try to draw a line with our personal lives, but more and more that line doesn't exist. So how do I protect my relationship without alienating my fans or being dishonest? I don't know. I haven't figured that out. Maybe I can't.

ENN: Let's set aside your personal life then, and the contract disputes, what can fans expect music-wise? Where would you like to go from here?

Grady Dawson: *I can promise that I'm not going to stop making music. You may have to find me on a street corner with an open guitar case at my feet [laughs] but I'll be there, singing my heart out like always. And I do actually want to say, on a personal note, that it means so much to me, the support and the belief my fans have given me, and I promise that I'll always believe in them, too. I won't let them down.*

30

Grady slides slowly into consciousness, aware only of
fingers winding through tendrils of his hair, a body warm and
firm beneath his cheek, the smell of sweet cedar and sharp citrus
and spicy cloves—Nico's cologne, he realizes, breathing deeply,
contented, burying his face in the warm skin of Nico's neck. They
so rarely get to wake up together like this, curled together in the
sleepy, safe harbor of their bed.

"Morning, gorgeous," Nico's even, pleasant voice says from above
him, low and hushed as if he's sharing a secret. It's then that Grady
remembers last night, what he heard, what Nico doesn't know that
he heard. Grady sits up and rubs the sleep from his eyes. Nico is
fully dressed except for his bare feet, and not just dressed but done
up as though they're hitting a red-carpet event, in a baby blue
seersucker suit with a pale yellow shirt, pink bowtie, and perfectly
folded pocket square. Grady has so many pressing questions, but all
he manages is "What—" before Nico stands and says, "I thought

we'd take Mom and Dad to a nice brunch before they head back to Sacramento. If that's okay with you."

That's right, they're leaving tonight on a red-eye. The last thing Grady wants is to ruin their last day here after they so kindly came all this way for him. The cancelled wedding discussion can be put on hold, so Grady ignores the nauseous pit in his stomach and says, "Yeah, that sounds good. But I don't want everyone to be bothered when we're out."

Nico tugs his coat flat and his tie tighter, then reaches up to check his hair. "Don't worry. I know this out-of-the-way place that should be perfect."

Grady showers and dresses and locks his heartbreak up tight; it's not the first time he's had to, so it's easy enough to emerge from their room with a smile on his face. In the living room, Nico and his parents are standing close together with their heads bent, intently discussing whatever Nico is showing them on his phone. They all look up and greet him in an unsettling, happy unison, "Good morning!"

"Well, look at you two," Grady says. Ken and Amy are just as dressed up as Nico, fancier than Grady's ever seen them. Ken is wearing a pale linen suit with his hair parted neatly, and Amy is in a light green gown and wearing makeup and has a blue origami-folded paper flower corsage on her wrist. Grady declares her the prettiest thing he's ever seen, and she giggles and swats at him. "Shall we?" he says, and offers Amy his arm. It's pleasant this morning; a tease of autumn catches on the breeze.

Parked in the driveway is a limo. Grady turns in confused silence to Nico, who shrugs as if taking a limo to brunch with his parents is a normal thing that he's completely unconcerned with—so much for worrying about money. "Didn't want to cram into my Miata or your truck, and the Belvedere doesn't have seat belts in the back."

A thirty-minute drive later, it seems as if Nico really meant it when he said "out-of-the-way." They go west off the highway, past the city limits toward Clay's house, through the blue-collar river-delta country towns, and then even farther, out where the restaurants are down-home Southern kitchens and not fancy brunch destinations. It's strange, and the way Nico is propped rigid and fretful on the edge of his seat is stranger, but Grady isn't in the mood to talk or suss things out, so he doesn't ask, just watches the road, just takes each moment as it comes. Then, just past a little downtown block and down the street from the car impound lot, the limousine stops.

Grady watches, completely stumped, as the driver opens the door and Amy and Ken get out. Nico moves to the seat across from Grady and puts his hands on Grady's knees. The limo door closes. "I have to come clean before we go in." Grady's heart thuds and skitters in his chest. He nods, because he can't speak. He braces himself, because he knows what's coming. This is it, then. "There is no brunch. And… I sort of bought this place."

"What?" Grady looks out of the window on the other side of the limo. It's that abandoned music store, now with the kudzu pulled off and the *For Sale* sign taken down. "I don't— I don't understand. What's going on?"

Nico squeezes Grady's knees, then wipes his own palms on his pants, leaving little damp spots on the crisp seersucker fabric. "Come inside, and I'll explain everything."

At the glass front door, Nico proudly brandishes a key, unlocks the door and opens it to a dim, wide-open empty room. He flips on the overhead florescent lights. Whatever he's doing here is mid-construction: the moldy carpet is only partly ripped up, the walls are gutted with gaping holes to get at the wiring and plumbing behind them, and the bathroom is in the middle of a total overhaul. There's framing up to separate the main sales floor from the back, splitting the large space in half, two-by-fours and plywood are piled in the front corner.

"I planned on being farther along in the process before I showed this to you," Nico says, "but you were getting suspicious, and it was only a matter of time before you figured it out. That guy you saw at my office wasn't maintenance looking at the pipes; he was a real estate agent. I've been going back and forth with him since we came here the first time."

That solves one mystery. "Why not just tell me, though?"

Nico pushes a hand though his perfectly swooped hair, lifts and drops his shoulders, then moves to the center of the room. "When you brought that old junk car home, I just— felt like a wet blanket about it, after. And I decided that I can be impulsive, too—" He places his thumb on his bottom lip and glances away. "If you can call weeks of scheming impulsive. I don't know. You do so much for other people, and you've put up with a lot of crap lately. I wanted to do something for you."

"You do plenty for me." Wedding or no wedding, that will always be true. And he gets it, he understands why Nico would want to back out; it's a lot to put up with.

"I wish I could make you believe that I'm not just grudgingly putting up with your life and everything that comes with it," Nico says. He frowns, then shakes his head. "Actually, I will in a bit. But first…" He comes back to take Grady's hand and leads him around the building. "So the idea was for you to have your own studio space. I don't know what will happen with the label, but I do know that you need a better space to work and record, and it's pretty much just two-by-fours right now, but this—" He sweeps his arm to indicate the area framed off in the back, "Will soon be your state-of-the-art private recording studio. I've been working with the guy who owns all the studios that Clem has been borrowing. I don't know if they're a thing or he's just someone else she's added to her dynasty. Either way he's been really helpful."

"Nico, I don't know what to say."

"That's okay; I'm not done." He tugs Grady back to the front, on a roll now, the place he thrives most: in charge. "Right here, this will be a stage. For, whatever. Just for fun or maybe open mic nights. I was thinking about what you said, the kids around here needing music. And I promise it won't smell like this forever." He wrinkles his nose. "I hope. Also I'm really seeing orange and yellow paint, hear me out: I know it's a little—"

Grady grabs his face and kisses him, hard. It effectively shuts him up, and Grady couldn't help it anyway. "Thank you. This is… You are… really incredible."

Nico grips Grady's wrists; his jaw is still cupped in Grady's palms. "Yeah?"

"Yeah." Grady kisses him again, then laughs. "Next time you don't have to be so secretive about it. Lordy. I mean for a second I thought you and Chet…" Grady wiggles his eyebrows suggestively.

"What? *No.* Grady, what kind of extremely low standards do you think I have? You saw his suit, right?" Nico clicks his tongue in disgust. "*Really.*"

"Just for a second!" Grady defends. "I know you wouldn't cheat on me, but you were skulking around like—" He remembers the phone call that had nothing to with buying this place, and his heart squeezes in his chest. "I heard you on the phone, cancelling the wedding venue." Nico drops his hands, steps back and away from Grady, and scrubs both hands through his hair.

"Oh. Well. About that."

This time Nico drags Grady to the very back to a storage room that's empty and narrow and dark, made of concrete and bare metal shelves with an industrial steel door. Nico keeps hold of his hand and with the other thumbs out a message on his phone; his face glows, drawn and intense, in the blue light. There's a blinding flash of sunlight, then the door slams closed with an echoing, scraping *thud*. Grady blinks to readjust his eyes to the dark; Spencer appears before him holding a two garment bags and two pairs of shining leather dress shoes.

"All set," Spencer says; he sounds out of breath.

"Excellent," Nico tells him. Then he says to Grady, "Come see."

Grady squints as Nico pushes the door open just a crack, and, as everything comes into focus, Grady knows for certain that this will be one of those moments that he will find imprinted on his memory forever, the kind that he'll close his eyes and relive over and over again.

The back parking lot is covered with a white tent covering a wonderland of natural wooden benches and twining tree branches. Green and white flowers hang from woven baskets strung along the edges; origami cranes and paper lanterns dangle from the branches. An aisle in the center is covered with green leaves that lead to an altar arched by green vines. It's the wedding venue they picked out and Nico cancelled, somehow picked up and placed in what was a cracked dirt parking lot.

"This is… What did you… How…" Grady splutters.

"I couldn't have pulled it off without Spencer. He's a miracle worker," Nico says.

"Bet you never thought you'd say that," Spencer says, not without some bite.

Nico snorts derisively. "Right?"

Grady shakes his head, stares at the tent and the magic inside, tries to make sense of it while his head spins and Spencer and Nico snark at each other like old friends. "But I don't—Today? You want to get married, here. Now."

Nico gives Spencer a silent signal, takes the garment bags and shoes and lets the door bang closed. "I know, I did it again, the steamrolling thing. I can't seem to help it. Are you angry?"

Grady blinks at him several times in the dark. "Angry?" He finally manages.

"Yeah, I—Listen. Everyone is at a bar down the street, and except for my parents and Spencer and Lucas, because he wouldn't fly out here unless I told him why, because he lives to make my life difficult like that—" He stops to rolls his eyes and sigh. "Other than that, no one knows they're here for a wedding. As far as they know, this a ribbon-cutting celebration for the new studio, and they're all waiting at the bar none the wiser." He pulls his spine straight and his jaw sets defiantly; that steely cool resolve is in full force. "You can say no."

All Grady can do is laugh. It's as if he's on a rollercoaster: everything is swooping and swaying; endorphins are buzzing; he's trying to catch his breath from the rise high to the top, the drop back down and then up, up again. When he gets his feet under him, he says to Nico's nervous face, "Are you ever gonna stop shocking the hell out of me?"

Nico breaks out into a wide toothy grin, his eyes crinkle, and he beams. "I certainly hope not." Grady steps forward to kiss him again, propelled by need and hunger. Nico stops him with a hand on the center of his chest. "Hold that thought. We need to get everyone here and get married. But first, we need to change."

Grady isn't *too* sad about waiting for that. "Hold on, aren't you already dressed up?"

Nico scoffs, "This is obviously my pre-wedding outfit. As if I would get married in seersucker." Grady is so glad he doesn't have to wait five more weeks to marry this man. Nico leaves to change in the gutted bathroom and pulls the string for an overhead lightbulb as he goes. Grady puts the garment bag and shoes on a less dusty section of a shelf and starts to undress. He's in only an undershirt, underwear, and black dress socks when there's a quick knock, followed by Gwen bouncing in and launching herself at him.

"I'm not decent!" Grady protests, laughing and scooping her up in a hug.

Gwen gives him a once-over. "I've seen way more than that. I mean your jogging shorts alone..." She bugs her eyes out; then Flora comes in and casts a sidelong glance at Gwen and does not look at Grady. She blindly holds out a granola bar that Grady gratefully scarfs down. He thought he was going to brunch; he's *starving.* "We've been informed that our groomsmaid services are required early."

"Looks like it." Grady pulls on the suit pants, while Gwen shakes out his button-down shirt. "Did you really not know?" he asks.

Flora smiles and shakes her head, and Gwen says, as she helps him put the shirt on, "I had an inkling that something was going on. He's been extra-stressed at work, coming in early and staying late. I've just been throwing kale salads and coffee at him and staying out of his way."

Grady doesn't know how Nico has managed it: working and arranging to buy this place and fix it up *and* planning a last-minute surprise wedding. On top of all of Grady's legal troubles and family drama, it doesn't seem fair; it seems so selfish of Grady to want more of Nico's time when he had so little of it to give.

Gwen helps Grady into his jacket, brushes down the sleeves and shoulders, and makes a small displeased noise. "Hey, Flor. In the trunk could you grab—"

"Your case with the steamer, yeah." Flora finishes for her, smiling sweetly at them before hustling to the parking lot.

"Got some wrinkles; can't have that. Your soon-to-be husband would shit a brick," Gwen says with an impish grin. Then Clementine appears, gliding into the storeroom and gushing, "You're getting married!" She presses two quick pecks to both of his cheeks. Flora comes back with the case, and the room is now very cramped with people and excited bustling about and chatter as he finishes getting ready.

"Wait." Grady has asked Flora, Clementine, and Gwen to be his best women, and he didn't even think about—"Who's with Nico?"

"I passed his brother on my way back in," Flora says, and, for a heart-stopping moment, Grady realizes that Lucas and Nico are alone in a very high-stress situation. Then Clementine adds, "A whole bunch of his family is here. Or, I'm assuming they're his family…"

"Yeah it is, some aunts and uncles and cousins from California," Gwen says. "Two of his cousins are with him and Lucas now." Gwen pauses and rocks up to her toes. "I'm realizing now that I should have suspected this was happening when he claimed his extended family came all the way out here for a new business venture." She shakes her head, then starts steaming his suit.

"And when he called us this morning and told us all to wear something light blue and 'summery semiformal,'" Clem says, complete with air quotes.

"Do we really find Nico telling us all what to wear *that* suspect, though?" Flora has a point everyone does have to agree with.

"I can't believe he went to all this trouble," Grady muses, holding his arms out so Gwen can steam him. "For me."

Gwen clicks off the steamer. "It's because he loves you, numbnuts. Now please tell me he remembered the cufflinks."

"He really does love you a lot," Flora says, in her soft, kind voice.

"God bless him," Clem adds with a wink.

Every moment after that is like a dream, one Grady has had so many times, wanting so badly to find that person who would look at him and want to keep him, and when he walks in from a side aisle he's afraid a too-strong intake of breath will send the dream swirling away like mist. A wedding photographer inconspicuously moves around to snap pictures. The music swells: Clementine's protégé musicians Ellis and Joaquin on acoustic guitar. Their family and their friends are all gathered here now: several members of Nico's extended family, with his parents right in front and Cayo settled on Amy's lap. To Grady's delight he spots Benny and a few other guys from the dirt bike track; Doris, the recently retired secretary from Stomp Records; Valencia and her daughter; the owners of his favorite record store; his favorite waitress from his favorite diner; the members of his band, of course, Billy, Mandy, Brad, and Mongo and their partners and families. Other musicians are here, too, and Spencer and Vince, so many faces that he encounters day-to-day, his community, his people. Grady's chest swells fit to bursting with love for all of them.

Then his heart stutters: There's another photographer with a reporter in the back, Hannah, the one who did his most recent magazine interview, and next to the reporter is his Uncle Clay. Next to Clay stands Lillian. Grady sways on his feet; then Nico is there, standing shoulder-to-shoulder with him at the arch made of vines. The minister raises her hands and starts, "Dearly beloved…" Blood whooshes in Grady's ears; vertigo captures him, *this is happening, this is happening, this is*— Nico takes his hand and squeezes. Grady's heart slows; his breathing deepens. This is happening.

When it's time for their vows, Nico goes a little stiff, pulls a folded piece of paper from his pocket, and turns bashfully to the audience. "I know everyone here is shocked that I struggled to come up with heartfelt sentiments," he jokes. Everyone chuckles, and, clearing his throat, he turns to Grady. "I'm not the romantic in this relationship, or the one who has a remarkable way with words. But I think you know what's in my heart, and will understand my clumsy attempts here." His suit is a contrast to Grady's; white pants to Grady's blue on darker blue on green plaid. Nico's coat is green, complemented by a tie and shirt both white with blue pinprick dots. Grady's shirt and tie are blue with blue stripes, and his suit coat is white. The effect is coordinating, not matching, with Grady's style more subdued and classic and Nico's a bolder step from tradition. It's perfect, of course.

"I guess what I want to say is that I hope you can see how loved you are," Nico looks out at the people gathered among the benches, then reads from the paper he holds with trembling hands. "I hope that right now you can feel some of the good you put out into the world reflected back at you. I have never met anyone who can take a punch and come up, not swinging, but smiling, quite like you can. At first I didn't quite get it." He blows out a breath and glances up at Grady before continuing. He's so damn beautiful, Grady is woozy with it. "But then I realized, you know what it's like to be hurt, and it doesn't make you angry or hateful, it just makes you kinder and more loving and more determined to make other people hurt a little less. Grady, you are the most compassionate, and *passionate*, person I have ever known, and I still can't quite believe that you picked me, of all people, to spend the rest of your life with."

Behind him the girls start to sniffle, and Nico's cousins wipe at their eyes; even Lucas looks moved. And if Grady can't kiss Nico soon, he'll go right out of his mind or pass out standing here in front of everyone so he blurts, "Can we get to the part where we're married yet?"

They audience laughs and cheers, and they do. They do.

Grady Dawson Ties the Knot. Get the exclusive photos and inside scoop here!
Entertainment News Now
by Hannah Jordan

Grady Dawson and celebrity stylist Nico Takahashi exchanged vows in a surprise ceremony just outside of Nashville on Sunday, and Entertainment News Now *got the exclusive invite. You're probably wondering why we got the chance to attend after the pair were so hush-hush about the engagement. As Nico told me at the downtown rooftop reception—where we were served gourmet sushi and mason jars of sweet tea—it's because, "Grady's fans loved him long before I came along, and I wanted to share some of our love with them in return. I can only be grateful for the support they've given him."*

To see what your support of Grady earned you, scroll down to see the photos we snapped of the ceremony, glamorous maid of honor

Clementine Campbell, the sealed-with-a-kiss I do's, the first dance, and the cutting of their wedding pie. Yes, pie.

Grady Dawson Takes On Stomp

StarzBuzz.com

The court date has been set for Grady Dawson's showdown with Stomp Records, coming just hours after he married his long-time stylist boyfriend in a secret surprise ceremony. Was the wedding rushed to take the heat off Grady and cast him in a positive light? The timing is hard to argue.

Stars at the Airport

StarzBuzz.com

Grady Dawson heads off on an international flight with new husband in tow. Honeymoon or running away from the controversy? What is your favorite airport look for Grady? Take our poll!

Somewhere in the Pacific Ocean, after taking a plane and a smaller plane and a boat, they are in a hut just off an island, where it seems as if the only thing that exists for days on end is their little thatched hut on stilts, him and Nico and a bed, and the endless blue sea all around them. "What do you want to do?" Grady asks, as he has every morning this week. He stretches his arms and legs and spine above the kicked-off covers. His bare skin is caressed by the breezy sea air, and he tastes salt on his lips when he licks them.

"Sleep," Nico says, still twisted halfway in the sheets. He's said that every morning so far, but soon he'll rouse lazily, call room service to order fruit and rice and fried plantains, and then consider scuba diving or hiking or renting a boat or just relaxing on the private beach. For now, he slips back into a peaceful sleep. Grady leaves him there, and pads across the bamboo floor of the hut to dive off the deck into the blue, blue ocean. And then he writes. Being so relaxed and at peace has released an easy flow of creativity; he'd worried, a bit, about losing his creative edge, that Stomp Records is right and no one wants to hear about his happiness. He's written from sadness and longing and heartbreak; if art comes from pain, then has he run out of things to say? But the scribbled words and notes and chords in his notebook and his voice and guitar carrying the rhythm of the waves say otherwise.

Nico blinks open hooded sleepy eyes, curls on his side, and watches Grady play his guitar and sing out on the deck before rising languidly from the bed. He slips on a satin robe and shuffles off to the bathroom. Grady plays a little louder while the water runs. The stronger late morning sun on the deck is turning Grady's shoulders and knees pink. When Nico returns from the bathroom, he's left the robe behind, and he settles back on the white linen sheets on his stomach, pillows his head on his bent arms, and looks at Grady from beneath his thick, dark lashes. Grady sets his guitar down and goes back to bed. He knows when he's being beckoned.

Grady starts with his mouth open against the dip of Nico's sacrum, kisses slowly up his spine and neck and curls his tongue around one warm earlobe.

Nico hums a sigh and says, "You smell like the ocean."

"Went for a swim," Grady replies, deep and husky. "I can shower." He nips the lobe with his front teeth.

Nico shivers. "No. You're— Good."

Grady mouths up the shell of his ear, then to a spot behind it, where Nico is so soft and sweet and hot, kisses along his jaw and neck and cranes to get at his mouth, then moves back down the same path. Nico smells like soap and shampoo and the salt in the air that's already clinging to his scrubbed-clean skin. Grady pauses at Nico's lower back where his spine ends, grasps both high, pert globes of his ass, and parts them. He waits for Nico to protest—only sometimes is he in the mood for this—and, when he doesn't, Grady drags his pointed tongue down the center of him.

Nico breathes out quiet moans; his hips grind a little on the mattress as Grady licks him. It's a mellower way of winding him up; he doesn't enjoy it quite as enthusiastically as Grady does. He does, however, suggest, "You should fuck me. I'm feeling lazy."

That he likes Grady to do even less often; it's harder for him to relax and he usually only wants Grady inside of him when he's half asleep and groggy, and even then will want Grady to hurry up and get it done with. "I'm happy right here," Grady says, with a broad swipe of his tongue against his hole. "We don't have to."

Nico pushes up on his elbows and twists around to send Grady a sharp look. "I want you to. Take a hint." He flicks his eyes up, then settles back down.

Grady laughs against his hot, smooth skin. "Yes, sir." But under Grady's tongue, Nico is too tight, too wound up. Grady pushes off the bed to find the honeymoon basket this resort was so kind to put in their room with that massage oil he's been wanting to try. Grady oils his hands, straddles Nico's waist, and digs his thumbs and fingertips into the tight muscles at the join of his shoulders and neck.

"*Oh, god,*" Nico says with a real, deep-chested groan. Grady massages his neck and all down his back, while Nico moans and goes lax beneath his hands. "I'd marry you twice if I could. God." Grady grins, kneading Nico's muscles until he's pliant; his lithe body is putty in Grady's hands. Then he scoots back, squeezes out more oil, and massages first Nico's lower back, then his glutes, then slips both slippery thumbs past the first rim of his hole.

"Okay?" Grady checks in; his breathing is picking up in time with Nico's. His thumbs slide out, back in, and Nico emphatically nods his head. His face is buried beneath one bent arm. Desire pulls tight in Grady's belly, his cock rises stiff and ready, but he isn't in a hurry. He bends and tastes Nico's skin while he carefully spreads him open. Grady's fingers are the waves lapping in and out; his lips and tongue are the lingering caress of the wind.

Nico is patient, too, only lifting his flushed face and gasping out, "please," when Grady settles his cock just once between Nico's cheeks. He pulls back, pressing the blunt tip where Nico is open now, wanting. But he hesitates, looking at Nico prone on the bed with his face hidden. Not like this. While Nico clumsily reaches for lube and condoms dropped onto the floor by the bed, Grady stretches out on his side, pulling Nico back against him.

This way he can kiss Nico's jaw and ear, can watch his lips part and eyes roll back as Grady first pushes in, can grab the inside of his thighs and his hip and pull as he inches in and in and slowly in. Can work Nico's cock in time with his long, slow thrusts.

The first time he touched Nico, the first time they made love, Grady wanted to saturate himself in it, wanted to draw it out as long as he could, because he was so sure it would be the last time, too. This moment is like that, and, just like then, no matter how much Grady tries to draw it out, take his time, and let their pleasure flow honey-slow and just as sweet, their bodies take over and demand more. Nico reaches back to twist his fingers tight in Grady's hair, grunts and curses and warns that he's close, "*so close, baby, please,*" and, in response, Grady's hips snap and his hand jacks faster and faster. Nico gets bumped up higher on the bed, causing Grady to be in danger of slipping out, so he releases Nico's cock to yank him back by the thigh, settles his ass snug in the bowl of Grady's hips, and drives in and in.

Nico takes his own cock in hand, then, and it's sexy enough watching him jerk himself off, but the glint of the wedding band on his finger as he does it sends Grady gasping over the edge. Nico comes over his own hand as Grady's hips still and his cock gives a few last pulses of release.

Grady catches his breath, gets rid of the condom, walks back on wobbly legs with a towel for Nico, and collapses back onto the mattress. "Now we nap," Nico says happily, and Grady can't imagine anywhere else on Earth he'd rather be than with this man, in this bed, in a thatched little hut on stilts stuck out somewhere in the wide blue sea.

33

One week later Grady is jolted back to reality when they hit a patch of turbulence in the air and the overhead seatbelt light flashes on. Grady pops his earbuds out and twists against the dull ache in his back.

"We're starting the descent soon," Nico says, scrolling through something on his tablet just the way he was before Grady went into his music trance. He doesn't know how Nico can sit still for so long.

"Thank the lord," Grady says, tucking one leg beneath him and shifting around. "What are you looking at?"

"Oh, some of those sites you hate, some fan forums." He powers the tablet down. "It's nice to read about everyone being happy for us. Mostly."

Grady rests his cheek on the seat back and smiles crookedly. "I'm happy for us, too. I still can't believe it."

Nico looks at his ring finger and spins the new wedding band with his thumb. The action sends a fierce rush of love and want through Grady.

"I can't, either," Nico says. "I can't believe I pulled it off, five weeks earlier than I planned."

"Wait, really?" Grady thought that the fake brunch and surprise wedding that day had been the plan all along.

Nico's eyebrows raise. "Well, you sprung my parents on me, and then I found out some fans had pinpointed the date. The CIA needs to hire fans for top secret intel, seriously. It was only a matter of time before my Plan B was discovered so—" The look he gives Grady is one of being defeated, but then it becomes bemused. "I know I was kind of being an asshole about the wedding planning and everything being perfect, but you weren't the only one who wanted to just get to the end part already."

Grady's chest beats with warmth. He takes Nico's hand and presses it to his mouth; the cool band is hard against his bottom lip. "It *was* perfect. Any wedding where I got to marry you would have been perfect."

"You know, you say these things, and what am I supposed to—" Nico shakes his head as though he can't cope, as though Grady is just *so much*, but not in a way that makes Grady feel bad about himself. He feels loved and wanted, officially and legally, and maybe it is just a piece of paper, their marriage license, but the message behind it is what matters: They went into this with eyes wide open, still chose each other, and promised to keep choosing each other, no matter what. Grady cups Nico's chin and pulls him in for a lingering, dragging kiss.

The turbulence settles, so the flight attendants make one last sweep of the cabin before they swoop down into Nashville. Their lunch dishes are cleared, and the attendant gives them each a gooey, fresh-baked cookie, which they tap together like champagne glasses.

"I may not be able to give up first class," Nico says, stretching his long legs in the generous space in front of him.

"We can use Clem's plane," Grady says between bites of chocolate chip cookie.

"Mmm, that's true," Nico replies. "We should probably let her know that she's taking us on as dependents should everything go to shit."

Grady chews slowly, furrowing his brows. "Do you think it will?"

"No," Nico brushes crumbs from his hands. "You know me; I need to be prepared for all eventualities." He does sort of have to be, in his line of work, Grady supposes.

"Maybe you're right about coming up from a hit," Grady says. What has his life been but a series of punches to the gut? He's always just figured he has two options: lie there in the dirt and give up, or dust himself off and keep going. And if he does it with a smile, well. "It's like Granddaddy used to say: *You can get glad in the same britches you got mad in.*"

Nico arches one eyebrow and sets his mouth flat. "What does that even... You know, even after living here, I still just do not understand the South." He sighs.

Grady gives him a sly grin. "Attitude is everything, sweetheart."

He's always believed from the beginning of this strange and surprising career of his that he's just a guy from a trailer park who picked up a guitar and got lucky. And if that luck runs out, well, he's got a lot going for him these days without it.

The day of the court date rolls around, and, when Grady comes out of the shower, Nico is setting out clothes on the bed. "Okay," he says not looking up, fluttering his hands over the clothes. "The idea is to look subdued and casual. The label's lawyers will all be wearing slick Italian suits; I'd put money on it. So you'll look like a humble, regular guy who got caught up with these sharks who just want to screw him over." He straightens and, almost manic with purpose, looks over at Grady. Then he narrows his eyes. "You're naked."

Grady looks down at himself, sets his hands on his naked hips and replies, "What do you want me to shower in? A scuba suit?" He smirks, making Nico huff and roll his eyes, so Grady sidles up close and tries to wiggle against him. "Am I distracting you?"

"We have to leave in thirty minutes, at the latest," Nico warns.

"That's plenty of time," Grady murmurs in his ear.

But Nico smacks his hip and darts away, points at Grady and reprimands, "Get dressed. Big day today."

The outfit is the sort of thing Grady would have worn to a court hearing before anyone knew his name and he'd have picked up new clothes at Sears for the occasion, which was likely Nico's exact intention. Plain white button-down, bland tie, khaki slacks. He could swear Nico once put a ban on any and all khaki in their home, yet here he is. He checks out Regular-Guy-Grady in the mirror and fiddles with his new hair cut; his curls are neat and short after Nico trimmed his hair last night. He's too restless to sit and wait, and after Nico denies him another attempt at fooling around to the take the edge off his nerves, he goes to the garage.

"No ATV, Grady. And don't get grease on those clothes," Nico calls after him, pulling the phone away from his ear and covering the end. "They aren't as cheap as they look." He moves the phone back in place and says into it, "Mom… They aren't going to let me livestream the proceedings for you… Yeah, I'll see what I can do."

Grady makes a cross over his heart, promising not to get too dirty. If he does get a little grease under his nails, it'll just help his image as an average Joe, right? In the end, he just sits on the Superbird's newly upholstered front seat after getting a text message from Lillian: *Helping Clay out next week after his surgery. Can I come by?*

Grady flips the phone over and over in his hand. He still doesn't know what do about her—how much to forgive, if he should. She's making amends and giving him space, and it's not fair for him to hold on to his resentment of her, only— It's all he's had of her for so long, his righteous anger. Vaughn is gone now, for good, and if she's gone, too, and he's given up his anger toward her, what would he have left?

"Grady?"

He looks up through the cracked windshield. "Flora, hey. I thought you and Gwen were meeting us at the courthouse." Grady starts to get out, but she walks over to the passenger side door and slides onto the bench seat next to him. "We are, I—" She rubs the shining white-leather seat with orange trim. "This is nice. The car's starting to come along." The new seat and rebuilt transmission are the only things nice about it so far.

"It's getting there," Grady says.

"Well. I came by to bring you this breakfast casserole." She lifts the casserole dish from her lap. "Gwen said that Nico makes sure that you eat when you're stressed, but that when *he's* stressed out, Gwen makes sure that Nico eats, and when *she's* stressed out I'm the one who makes sure Gwen eats, and— I was up half the night worrying about no one eating a proper breakfast and woke up at four to make two breakfast casseroles. It's the Italian grandmother in me, I guess."

"It's the mom in you." Grady takes the casserole dish and smiles. "Thanks, Flora." He hasn't eaten; he's been too anxious, and Nico is more coffee than man by now. The casserole smells divine. He tells Flora that, and she ducks her head and blushes.

"So does this thing run?" She asks, tugging her braid over her shoulder and fiddling with the end of it. The transmission works now, and he's figured out how to rig the starter and alternator to turn the engine over.

"Sorta. It has no brakes and overheats after about thirty seconds, but in theory, yeah."

Flora nods. "Still. Most people would have just left it to rot. And you got it working."

"Most people are smarter than me," Grady says with a chuckle. Flora goes quiet, tugging at her braid, and, though Grady's stomach gurgles its interest in the breakfast casserole, he waits for whatever she's wanting to say.

"Cayo's birth mother contacted us," she says softly. "I think that's why I— pushed you, kind of, to reach out to your mother. I was projecting a bit. And I wanted to apologize. For that."

"You don't have anything to apologize for." They are two different situations entirely, Cayo's very wanted adoption and his almost-literal drop on his grandparents' doorstep. "What does she want?"

"Just pictures and updates, occasionally. All through the social worker, of course. It sounds like she's in a better place now. So that's good." Flora's fingers wind around the end of her braid. "It's complicated, the idea of sharing him like that. We want him to know her, but there's this fear of rejection, too. For us, because she'll always be part of him, and we don't want him to think we've kept that from him. And for her, that maybe he'll want nothing to do with her. And that's okay." Her hands pause on her braid as she nods. "It's okay if his feelings are complicated. I hope he knows, at least, that we only ever want the best for him, and that it takes a tremendous amount of bravery to admit that what's best for your child may not be you."

Grady looks at the black, silent screen of his phone, and they sit without speaking in his junk pile of a car, a car that a person with any sense would have walked away from and never looked back. Maybe it never will be what it should have been—too many years of neglect, too many rusted out parts—but it can still be something. The frame is good; there are parts that can be salvaged. He takes Flora's anxious hand and holds on until Nico comes to collect him.

"It's time."

On any other day, Grady appreciates the architecture of the stately white stone antebellum-style courthouse with its huge bronze doors and stained-glass windows. But today the imposing building just adds to his sense of dread. His career and financial future are on the line, and he'll be okay whatever happens; he'll build back up from nothing because he has before, and he'll do it with the support of his family and friends and fans, but he sure as hell doesn't *want* to. The reporters and cameras are only allowed as far as the front steps, and Grady keeps his head down, tries to look serious but not angry the way his lawyer, Ms. Howard, said before she led him at a clipped pace past the gently dancing fountains and through the crowd. "No comment," she keeps saying on his behalf, and then Grady recognizes the reporter, Hannah, who came to the wedding and interviewed him at the house and once before that. He's always really liked her; she's clever and sweet and genuine.

"Grady, can you give us a quick statement?"

"No comment at this time," Ms. Howard says.

"Wait, hold on a sec." Grady speaks into the recorder Hannah is holding toward him. "I just want to say…" Grady glances at Ms. Howard, who sets her mouth in concern, but does tip her chin with consent. "Whatever happens in there— All I ever wanted to do was make good, honest music. I never had any expectation of fame or fortune or anything like that. So if the rest of it all goes away, then, then I'm just gonna keep on making good honest music. And I—" He stops to take Nico's hand, in full view of the crowd and the press and the cameras. "Nico and I appreciate everyone who has supported us; it really means a lot to us both. That's all."

Then he's whisked inside, through marble hallways on shining polished wood floors under tall arching ceilings with bronze chandeliers and stone carvings. Grady ducks into the bathroom that's hidden behind a statue of a lioness; her somber stone eyes follow him until he's out of sight. He splashes water on his face, pats his cheeks dry with a paper towel, and says to the pale, panicked Grady in the mirror, "You're gonna be okay. Whatever happens, you're gonna be okay." Someone flushes a urinal behind him, then a man in a nice suit washes his hands next to Grady as nonchalantly as if he sees people giving themselves desperate pep talks in the courthouse restroom mirror every day. He looks like a lawyer, so maybe he does. Lawyer-guy leaves, and then Nico comes in.

"Holding up okay?" Nico's voice is tight, his body and face are nothing but rigid, sharp edges. Grady's guilt over dragging him through this returns, until Nico slides off his own stylish sports coat. "The regular guy approach is good, but Gwen pointed out that it was maybe too casual." He helps Grady into the coat, tugs the lapels, and buttons the two bottom buttons. "Now, no more freaking out. You're not in the wrong. I'm happy to be standing by you. Everything is going to work out."

He's obviously convincing himself as much as he is Grady, so Grady takes a breath and nods. "Okay." Grady checks himself in the mirror one last time. The coat does make him look more put together, though it's a little too snug in the arms and chest. It beats the first time he had to do something like this, when he borrowed his Granddaddy's church suit that was way too big and threadbare at the knees and elbows. "This is not my first trial, did you know that?"

"I may have heard rumors of the sort," Nico says with clear distaste.

Shame weighs in his belly as Grady lists, "Driving under the influence. Drug possession. Trespassing and damaging private property, and… Mm. Resisting arrest, I think was the official accusation."

Nico's face is unreadable; he fixes the knot on Grady's tie that doesn't need to be fixed. "Must have been a wild night," he finally says.

Grady's laugh is a grateful release of tension. "It was a few separate occasions. In case you ever wondered why I don't drink." He tries to play it off as a joke, though not a bit of it is actually funny.

"I know who I married," Nico runs his hands down the satin material of Grady's tie. "Warts and all. Metaphorical warts, of course. If you had real ones, well." He makes a *no way* face. Grady laughs again, feels lighter again. "I'm not a total Boy Scout, you know. I've been to Tijuana on spring break. I've done things."

Grady squints at him. "You were a Boy Scout, though. I saw the photo albums."

"A *metaphorical* Boy Scout," Nico says with a sigh and flickering roll of his eyes. "All right, Grady Dawson, menace to society. Let's do this."

In the courtroom, Nico joins Flora, Gwen, Clementine, and Spencer in the audience, and Grady sits at a large table up front to the left; at the table on the right is Duke, bracketed by a team of lawyers in slick charcoal suits, just as Nico predicted. Throughout the hearing, none of them spare Grady a glance. Has he ever been anything other than a chain of dollar signs to Stomp Records? It's hard for him to believe that.

Ms. Howard went through what the proceeding would be like a few days ago: Stomp would present their case, then she would present his case, then the judge will take some time to review each side and make his or her decision. It's an arbitration and not a criminal trial, so Grady won't have to take the stand or be cross-examined. "It'll be boring, overall," she said. But Grady's heart is trying to gallop right out of his chest no matter what she told him.

The judge doesn't take very long to come back with a decision, which makes Grady's lawyer sit very straight very fast, and makes Grady's pounding heart leap into his throat. The judge hands down her decision, taps her papers into a pile, and smacks the gavel down. Case closed. Just outside the courtroom, Grady drops back against the cold marble wall as everyone who came along to support him gathers around. Then Stomp's gang of lawyers marches past, and Duke Delmont stops to shake Grady's hand. "No hard feelings, son."

Nico tips his head, works his jaw, and crosses his arms over his chest. Gwen *hah's* so loudly it echoes through the chamber. Flora glowers, and Spencer's glare could be a death stare.

"You got a lot of balls, Delmont," Clem says. Grady looks at this man, who he thought was an ally, a friend, and sees what he really is with his gold rings and gaudy belt buckles and loud bluster: a guy who's trying way too hard to believe he matters. He's just as much a cog in the machine as Grady is—a filthy rich cog, but still a cog.

"You know what, Duke," Grady says, gripping Duke's hand with both of his in a firm handshake. "No hard feelings." He releases Duke's hand and adds in an icy, passive-aggressive tone of voice that would have made Memaw beam with pride, "May god bless your soul."

Court Rules in Favor of Grady Dawson:
Says Not in Violation of Contract, Is Free to Record at Another Label.
Nashville Indy Press
Blake Davidson reporting

A Nashville court declared that Grady Dawson is no longer bound by his contract with Stomp Records, denying the label's claim that Dawson violated the terms by not providing an appropriate album and by performing an unreleased song in public. Stomp Records was also seeking to reinstate the initial three-record, seven-year contract due to these claims.

"Stomp Records was really only seeking to keep Grady Dawson a prisoner of the label," Dawson's manager Vince Bauer told press. "Making up claims and violations that Grady would never commit. They have their album, they know full well the content of Grady's character, and the judge could see that clearly."

Entertainment Attorney Tanisha Howard represented Dawson, while the case for Stomp Records was pled by the law firm Hickey, Hickey and Bloodworth. Dawson looked dressed down and somber while walking into the courtroom, but returned jubilant and visibly relieved, hand in hand with his new husband, a marriage which some say was the real source of the controversy with Stomp all along. Now released from Stomp Records, Dawson says he will be considering his options for a new label, but said in a statement that he, "Can't wait to make new music. I feel free, like I'm only just getting started."

35

Grady had met Nico only thanks to Spencer. But Grady blew his chance, tongue-tied at the sight of Nico, while smack in the middle of an interview. He'd been rapidly losing patience and an ability to focus on the questions:

"Rumors say that you—"

"We hear you're dating—"

"What parties will you be—"

Red carpets are a loud, stiflingly hot chaos of flashing cameras and dozens of concurrent interviews, of last-minute primping and briefings and making sure to be seen with the right people at the right time. Whatever that particular interviewer was asking Grady got sucked into the vortex of it all when a waif-like model swept into Grady's peripheral vision, trailed by a harassed-looking stylist. The model may have been the one gracing runways and magazine covers, but it was the stylist Grady couldn't take his eyes off.

"Excuse me." Grady stepped away mid-interview. He knew it was rude and he'd hear about it later from Vince, but, whoever that guy was, with his striking features and perfect hair and legs for days, he was elegant and regal even while sniping at the model to get over herself. Whoever he was, Grady needed to know. And then the guy flipped to a genuine concern and gave the insecure-masking-as-bravado model a pep talk, told her she was beautiful and she was strong, and Grady couldn't live another moment without talking to him.

But then another microphone appeared, and the crowd closed in, cutting off his intended path. He felt the chord of connection between him and the mysterious stylist was severed. That was it, he'd lost his chance and he knew, he just *knew*, there was something there, something important.

"I'll set up a meeting." Spencer sighed and scowled. "Despite my better judgment." It would not be the first time Spencer had helped him set up a "meeting."

"I'm done with hookups," Grady reminded him. He was tired of it, tired of being that guy, and it led nowhere but disappointment and depression and a distraction from his career goals. He wasn't gonna to find love in the bed of a stranger; he just wished it hadn't taken him so long to sort that out.

Spencer replied with a skeptical grunt. "We'll see. What did the model look like?"

"I dunno, a model. Tall. Skinny. I wasn't really paying close attention."

Spencer gave him another long-suffering sigh. "What was she wearing?"

Luckily Grady remembered the gown, mostly because he'd watched her stylist adjust and fluff and fold and fuss over it. It was gold, with pleats as sharp as his jawline and accents of swirling velvet as black as his hair. And somehow, from that, Spencer found him and then called and bullied his way into a meeting in the very short time Grady would be in L.A.

"Spence…" Grady warned when a sneering Spencer hung up the phone. They'd talked about that before. Spencer didn't know the strength of his own assertive nature sometimes.

"I just wanted to make sure it happened," Spencer protested. "I can tell that you like him and—" His shoulders slumped; his defensiveness ebbed away. "Be careful, okay? I don't want you to get hurt."

Spencer was a good assistant because he was determined and sure, a little foolhardy, but it worked out for the best, usually. And he didn't just do things because he had to, but because he cared. "I will be."

Today, Grady climbs the steps to Nico's office just as he had that afternoon back in L.A. He'd taken a slow jog twice around the block then to calm his nerves and still pushed the door open with sweaty palms and a fluttering stomach, and today, just like then, it's Gwen who greets him. Only now, it's with a smile and a wave instead of a deliberate drag of her eyes up and down him from head to toe and back and then declaring, "Oh, this is gonna be fun." Grady liked her instantly.

Today, Gwen has Cayo on her lap and she only has eyes for that little boy. "This is our new assistant," she says, ruffling his hair. Cayo chews on a capped pen, watching a video on her computer screen as she works on a look-book; the show sounds like *Sesame Street*. From her lap Cayo notices Grady and yells, "Dee Dee!" Grady points to himself, and Cayo says it again. "Yeah, that's your name now," Gwen says, "deal with it."

Grady will not just deal with it; he loves it. He crouches for a chat, until Cayo is entranced by Elmo and Mr. Noodle again, so

Grady stands and turns to talk to Spencer, who isn't there. Grady nods his head to indicate the empty receptionist's desk, "Where's your old assistant? I have exciting news, I wanted to tell all y'all."

"Spencer quit," Gwen says simply.

"Again?" Grady stands up, frowning at the abandoned desk. He doesn't know how to help Spencer sometimes, not when he keeps running out ahead of himself and worrying about the consequences later. Grady feels like a father with wayward teenager. He has a moment of sympathy for what he put his grandparents through, what his mother put his grandparents through. The door opens, and Nico comes in with a few shopping bags. He puts them on the stairs to the loft so he can greet Grady with a peck on the lips.

"Nico!" Cayo exclaims, holding his little arms out.

"Okay, how does he say your name perfectly?" Grady asks.

Nico scoops Cayo up into his arms. "We worked on it, didn't we? I could not abide being called Uncle Igo." Cayo babbles something back at him.

Grady knows that Gwen brings Cayo into the office from time to time, especially now that it's late fall and Flora is back to work, Cayo back to daycare, and Gwen's hours are as odd and unpredictable as ever. They're making it work, though, and Cayo is a big, healthy toddler with a friendly, upbeat personality. It seems that his charming temperament finally won Nico over.

"All right, back to Mommy," Nico says. "I need to log that stuff now that we're out an assistant, again."

"Still waiting on that errand boy," Gwen remarks as Nico heads over to the stairs.

"What happened with Spencer?" Grady follows. He and Nico seemed to be getting along, but it was probably only a matter of time before their dueling headstrong natures caused problems again.

"Oh, it was a mutual parting of ways," Nico replies, scooping up the bags. "He found his calling, he says. Wedding planning." Nico pauses halfway up the staircase to add, "Gwen, what did he say? About the... wedding romp? Is that what he called it?"

Gwen leans back, covering Cayo's ears. "One hundred percent wedding hookup rate for him so far. I do believe he called it the 'booty bonus.'"

Nico *tsks*. "That's right," he says, voice crisp.

Grady follows him to the loft, where Nico starts pulling clothes and jewelry from the bags and setting receipts aside. "Well, good for him," Grady says, "Wait. Who did he hook up with at our wedding?" A one hundred percent hookup rate—when did Spencer turn into such a stud? Grady will have to talk to him about making sure he's not looking for love in all the wrong places.

"It was uh—" Nico snaps his fingers and looks up, trying to remember. "The guy from the bike track. Ugh, what's his name— Cute face. Tattoos on his arms. Says 'yo' a lot. I just described three-fourths of the kids who hang out there," Nico says with a glance upward.

"Benny?" Grady questions. Nico points at him in affirmation. Grady had no idea. "Huh, what do you know."

"Anyway," Nico says, hanging a leather jacket on a garment rack. "He'll still be around some. We're letting him use the office as a home base for now; we've been tossing around the idea of offering personal stylist services for weddings. Expand a little."

Grady hands him a pair of black pants and a red shirt so he doesn't have to keep walking back and forth across the loft. "Do you have time for that?"

"Well," Nico says making sure everything is hung neatly and the hangers are evenly spaced. "You're focused on writing songs and getting the studio up and running, and I think we've realized that I boss you around enough at home, so it's probably best to let Gwen take over all of your styling. And Clementine... What Clementine is really up to is anyone's guess. She's still committed to the careers of Ellis and Joaquin and now a few more kids still hoping to make it big, but she's been extra cagey about what she's filling her days with other than that."

"She'll come out of hiding soon enough," Grady says.

Nico lifts his shoulders. "Until she does, gotta keep hustling, you know. Speaking of. Are you going by the studio later?"

Oh yes, his news—he got way off track, what with Spencer's new career and surprising hookups. "Yeah, actually. I have exciting news. I'll show you."

"Well?" Grady asks, sweeping both arms out and stepping back, nearly turning his ankle on a pothole. They'll need to repave the parking lot sooner rather than later. At least the weeds were pulled, all the trash and debris cleared away, and the exterior of the building power washed. And now, there's the new sign on the awning that looks fantastic.

"Spotlight Studios. I like it," Nico says. "The place is looking less and less like the scene of a final showdown between zombies and a ragtag group of survivors."

Grady laughs, "Right on. Okay, there's more." He leads the way inside the old music store, and though it's not finished yet, not by a long shot, it is finally starting to take the shape of the vision Grady has for it. He has been spending a lot of time composing and writing, and getting the songs release-ready, but he's been here a lot, too, planning, guiding, and picking up a hammer to bring his vision to life with his own two hands.

"So, the stage just needs lighting work now, and we've left this whole wide space for the audience." Grady walks backward and indicates the wide open floor in the front of the studio. "And it seemed like such a waste of space, just leaving it empty except for open mic nights." Grady presses his palms on the back wall; thick foam sound panels have been installed all around the space to keep open mic night from disturbing the nearby residences and businesses, but the ones on the back wall—

Grady lifts one panel, and a tripod kicks out beneath it. "Cool, right?" He sets four of the movable panels to configure a cozy, high-walled, sound-absorbing cubicle. "It was Clay's idea." He's been here helping out a lot, ignoring Grady's concerns about his knees and overdoing it, until just recently, when he was forced to take a break for his replacement surgery and recovery.

"Yeah, but what is it for, exactly?" Nico smooths his hands over the outside of the foam cubicle. "You starting a telemarketing business? We're doing okay now, financially. You know that right?" He knocks on a panel; it barely makes a sound. "Saved a ton on the wedding by having it in a parking lot."

"Hah! No. I was thinking about what Clem is doing with the kids lookin' to make it in the business who might not have a chance. Like maybe I could do that, too, so I'm offering the studio for that." He nods toward the far left corner, where the glass-walled recording area is very nearly finished. "But then it's like— What about the kids who can't even get that far? I mean, if someone hadn't put a guitar in my hands and believed in me long before I set foot in Nashville, I wouldn't be here at all. So I want to offer music lessons. Scholarships or sliding scale or— I dunno. I'm not a business guy, but—" Grady finishes with a shrug. He'll figure something out.

Nico searches his face and rests his thumb against his bottom lip the way he does when he's considering something before speaking. "I'll call Lucas. He'll know how to arrange all of that on the up and up. And Dad gives free haircuts, just once a year at back-to-school time. Though Mom handles that stuff..." He looks around. The wheels are almost visibly whirring in his head. "I wonder if we can make the whole thing a nonprofit, actually. Hmm."

"All right, before you get too carried away, there's one more thing." Grady arcs his hand, palm up, to the door down the hall, on the right. "Step into my office, please."

His office was the back storage area and it's still all concrete and smells of mildew. They've replaced the heavy steel door with light-weight Masonite; its etched glass panels and the new track lighting make the space much less mausoleum-like. Grady sits in his new office chair at his new desk. He never really saw himself as a desk guy, but he doesn't mind this. "Have a seat," he says to Nico, and gives a lopsided smile when Nico primly crosses his legs and arches an eyebrow.

"So. Can you pencil me into your busy schedule?" he says, dipping his chin and batting his eyelashes.

Grady barks a laugh and then pretends to page through a pile of papers. He only has a few papers, really, and he slides one of them to Nico. "I don't know. I'm awful busy. Little pushy, to demand I just fit you in like that with so little notice."

Nico taps his finger on his lips. "I mean, who would *do* such a thing, right?" They hold heated, flirting eye contact, then Grady breaks it to look pointedly at the paper he put right under Nico's nose, but Nico is far too busy giving Grady bedroom eyes to look down. Normally, Grady wouldn't say no to that, and there is the matter of officially christening his new office, but— "Nico, look at the paper," Grady says with a laugh.

"What? Oh." Nico blinks back into awareness, then picks up the paper and reads, lips pulled in and eyebrows low. "This is…" He looks at Grady from behind the paper. "This is a contract."

Grady bounces in his seat, he's so stoked. "Yep. I signed with Sovereign Records. They're an independent label. Signed Ellis and Joaquin, too. They're new, but really committed to bringing unique voices to Nashville and supporting queer artists. And look at who's on the letterhead."

Nico squints and looks back at the contract. "Clementine Campbell. I should have known." He shakes his head. "This is the one that was courting you recently, right? Wait, did you know when you signed?"

"Nope." She sent an agent, who wined and dined him and everything. Of course, if he knew it was Clem who started this new label, he would have signed automatically. That's likely why she didn't tell him, and he's glad he made the decision with a clear head and no outside pressure. Sovereign wants to release "Blended Notes" right away, on the album Stomp declined, and then "By the Bye" and all the others he's been working on while waiting for things to settle. They wanted all of his music, not reluctantly or with grudging acceptance that isn't acceptance at all, but enthusiastically.

When he finally talked to Clem about it and asked how she managed to get out of her own contract at a different label, she winked and said simply, "I just asked real nice, sugar."

The downside of a smaller independent label is lack of clout, even with Clementine as the force behind it, but the benefit of creative freedom far outweighs any fame or big-league dealings for Grady. Nico moves around the desk, lands in Grady's lap, and cups his chin to kiss him. Grady scoots the chair back, situates Nico's ass into a more pleasing position, and then he remembers.

"Shoot, Clay's coming by to start installing the stage lights." Grady checks the time and, unfortunately, has to nudge Nico off of his lap. Clay's got the go-ahead from his doctor to get back to work; he called Grady from the parking lot at the doctor's office with the news. The poor guy must have been going stir crazy. He comes at the exact time he said he'd arrive, pulls up in Vaughn's now-working car, and walks in leaning on a cane, but getting around much faster and easier than before.

Grady greets him with a handshake and a squeeze to his shoulder. "How're the new knees doing?"

Clay sets the cane aside, secures his tool belt, and says with a flat tone, "All right." He limps off to get to work. After all the time he and Grady have spent together here, he's still a man of very few words. But he shows up, and that's all that matters. On this occasion, though, Grady would have preferred a little communication, because Clay didn't come alone. Lillian is hovering by the doorway.

She lifts a hand. "Hey, Grady."

Nico says hello to her, asks how she's been, and the whole time they talk she keeps sending Grady furtive, nervous glances. It's as if he's a snarling stray dog that she's afraid to approach lest she get bitten. Grady regrets that he's made her feel that way, though he's certainly had his reasons for being angry and guarded. Maybe those reasons don't matter so much anymore.

"I need to get back to work," Nico announces. "Unless you need me to... *help* with anything." He darts an obvious look toward Lillian.

"No, that's okay. I'll meet you at Flora and Gwen's for dinner, all right?" Grady kisses Nico's cheek, and Nico leaves after a lingering squeeze of Grady's hands. Then, to Lillian, Grady says, "I didn't know you were in town."

She scratches at some of the peeling black paint on the doorway. "I, uh, he needed some help after his surgery, though he's so stubborn about it—" A fleck of paint chips off, landing on one of her sneakers. "We're not technically kin, you know. But he's alone and he's been there for me like family, so I wanted to do the same for once."

She starts on another peeling patch of paint; the whole thing needs to be painted. Grady bets if he let her stand there and stew for long enough she'd strip the whole thing and save him the hassle. There's something he's been putting off doing though, somewhere he thought he'd need to go alone. "Would you come with me for bit?"

Grady explains as they pull out of the parking lot that they're shooting the cover for his next album at the trailer park where he grew up. They have permission and permits, but he wants to scout it himself first and feel whatever he needs to feel without a photographer and crew and makeup artists tagging along. Then the silence is like a third person taking up all of the space between them on the bench seat of Grady's truck.

Halfway there Grady asks, "How've you been?"

"Still sober. I know that's what you're really asking." The uncomfortable silence pushes them even farther apart for the second half of the trip.

The trailer park has a new swing set, and they finally patched up the section of fence that looked as if a car plowed through it. Mostly, though, the place looks the same as ever. It's always been worn and tired and broken down, as if it started out of the gate defeated, but to Grady it looks like home, like simplicity, like honest hard-working people just trying their best. No one is home at their old trailer, so Grady parks in the driveway and hops out.

"I haven't been here in a long time," Lillian says when she comes to stand against the truck bed next to him. "Since after her funeral." Her voice wavers. When Grady looks, he can see that her face is drained of color. He starts to suggest that they go, that this was a bad idea, but then she continues in the same trembling voice, "I remember you were there and I couldn't even comfort you I was so out my head with grief. Then I left because all I wanted was to disappear. I deserved to disappear. I punished myself for so long."

Grady moves incrementally closer to her. "I did, too. I blamed myself."

She releases a heavy breath. "This is harder than I thought it would be."

"We can go, I— I come back here from time to time. I can feel them here, never did when I went out to their graves."

"No," she says, voice a little steadier. "I've needed to do this for a long time."

They stand quietly, facing the old trailer. It has a newer porch now, and the eaves and skirting were long ago stripped bare of Memaw's flowers, wind chimes, and holiday-appropriate flags. There's the dent still on the aluminum siding just off the porch where Grady used to throw his bike, and the warped gutter over his bedroom window that would rush like a waterfall during heavy rain is still warped as ever. Grady can close his eyes and almost hear Memaw hollering to him for dinner, his steps as he runs past Granddaddy cursing up a storm at his finicky old car, the screen door screeching closed behind him, the hollow pattering of his feet across the kitchen. Grady would have likely had a skinned knee, wild hair, and even wilder peals of laughter.

The idea for the album cover was simple: Start at the beginning, a symbol of tenacity and strength of spirit, of achieving his dreams but never forgetting who he is or who helped him get there. Lillian is still sniffling and pale as a ghost, so Grady says, because maybe she needs to hear it, "I was happy here. I had a good life, I felt safe and loved. I was happy, really."

Sorrow breaks across her face, and tears fall in splotches into the dirt at their feet. "Good. That's— I'm really glad." Her eyes dart over his face and his hair, as if she's seeing something there she can't quite make sense of. "I'm sorry," she says, looking away and swiping at her cheeks. "You just— You look—"

"So much like him, yeah." It doesn't feel like a kick in the gut anymore; he's made his peace with it, as much as he can. He wishes only that Vaughn had the chance to find some peace in his own life, before it was too late.

"You remind me of him, too," Lillian says, and Grady's face must twist into something awful because she quickly adds, "In a good way. Vaughn was the kind of person who walked into a room and commanded everyone's attention like a magnet made of charisma." She shifts to face him, propping her arm on the edge of the truck bed. "So many people loved him, but he never believed them; he wouldn't take it. Not like you. I've watched you, I've seen you take the love everyone gives you and send it back even stronger. You're the best of him, Grady." She looks at the trailer. "You're the best of them. And I'm sorry it took me so long to get here, but I am..." She wavers out a breath. "I am trying."

Grady swallows the lump in his throat. For so long all he had of her was the way she left him behind, he had to harden his heart to her. He came to believe that he always would be left behind, that everyone in his life was going to leave in the end and he had to be okay with that. And now—he is so loved, isn't he? Not just Nico, but so many people love him and he loves them just as much.

"I think you're in there, too," Grady finally says. "I must have gotten all my blind, stubborn optimism from somewhere."

She smiles, watery and crooked, but with a hint of sunshine. "Oh, I don't know—"

"You're here aren't you? Still standing." Standing with a heart chipped and cracked and stitched back together, a soul charred at the edges from the burns suffered along the way, a life of shattered, scattered bits gathered up and blended into something odd and unusual and unexpected, but whole. Still whole, still standing, still here. And now—he climbs in the truck with his mama, with clouds of dirt flying behind them and taillights flashing at the stop sign. He's heading home to his husband, his friends, his family, to his perfect, messy, chaotic life—now no longer alone.

The End

ACKNOWLEDGMENTS

Thank you to everyone who believes in me, encourages me, and loves me (you know who you are). This book would not exist without you. I hope that I'm able to take some of that love and encouragement and kindness and send it back out into the world even stronger. That's all I've ever wanted to do.

ABOUT THE AUTHOR

Lilah Suzanne has been writing actively since the sixth grade, when a literary magazine published her essay about an uncle who lost his life to AIDS. A freelance writer from North Carolina, she spends most of her time behind a computer screen, but on the rare occasion she ventures outside she enjoys museums, libraries, live concerts, and quiet walks in the woods. Lilah is the author of the Interlude Press books *Spice*, *Pivot and Slip*, *Broken Records*, and *Burning Tracks*.

To sign up for Lilah's monthly newsletter for exclusive content, free stories and updates, visit lilahsuzanne.com.

also from **lilah suzanne**

Broken Records, Spotlight Series Book 1

Los Angeles-based stylist Nico Takahashi loves his job—or at least, he used to. Feeling fed up and exhausted from the cutthroat, gossip-fueled business of Hollywood, Nico daydreams about packing it all in and leaving for good. So when Grady Dawson—sexy country music star and rumored playboy—asks Nico to style him, Nico is reluctant. But after styling a career-changing photo shoot, Nico follows Grady to Nashville where he finds it increasingly difficult to resist Grady's charms.

ISBN (print) 978-1-941530-57-3 | (eBook) 978-1-941530-58-0

Burning Tracks, Spotlight Series Book 2

In the sequel to Broken Records, Gwen Pasternak has it all: a job she loves as a celebrity stylist and a beautiful wife, Flora. But as her excitement in working with country music superstar Clementine Campbell grows, Gwen second-guesses her quiet domestic bliss. Meanwhile, her business partner, Nico Takahashi and his partner, reformed bad-boy musician Grady Dawson, face uncertainties of their own.

ISBN (print) 978-1-941530-99-3 | (eBook) 978-1-945053-00-9

After the Sunset

An Interlude Press Short Story

Caleb Harris and Ty Smith-Santos have never crossed paths until they learn that a farm in Sunset Hallow, Washington has been bequeathed to both of them. They prepare to sell the farmhouse, but soon find themselves falling for the charming farm, the lonely man who left it to them, and each other..

ISBN (eBook) 978-1-945053-49-8

Spice

In his Ask Eros advice column, Simon Beck has an answer to every relationship question his readers can throw at him. But in his life, the answers are a little more elusive—until he meets the newest and cutest member of his company's computer support team. Simon may be charmed, but will Benji help him answer the one relationship question that's always stumped him: how to know he's met Mr. Right?

ISBN (print) 978-1-941530-25-2 | (eBook) 978-1-941530-26-9

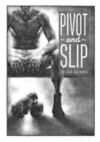

Pivot and Slip

Former Olympic hopeful Jack Douglas traded competitive swimming for professional yoga and never looked back. When handsome pro boxer Felix Montero mistakenly registers for his yoga for Seniors class, Jack takes an active interest both in Felix's struggles to manage stress and in his heart and discovers along the way that he may have healing of his own to do.

ISBN (print) 978-1-941530-03-0 | (eBook) 978-1-941530-12-2

One **story**
can change **everything.**

@interlude**press**

For a reader's guide to **Blended Notes** *and book club prompts,*
please visit interludepress.com.

CPSIA information can be obtained
at www.ICGtesting.com
Printed in the USA
FFOW03n0817231017
41337FF